My Woman
His Wife

My Woman His Wife

A Novel by
Anna J.

Q-Boro Books
WWW.QBOROBOOKS.COM

An Urban Entertainment Company.

ISBN 978-0-7394-7566-9

This is a work of fiction. It is not meant to depict, portray or represent any particular real persons. All the characters, incidents and dialogues are the products of the author's imagination and are not to be construed as real. Any references or similarities to actual events, entities, real people, living or dead, or to real locales are intended to give the novel a sense of reality. Any similarity in other names, characters, entities, places and incidents is entirely coincidental.

Cover Photo & Art—Copyright © 2004 by Q-BORO BOOKS all rights reserved
Cover Concept—Jamel Johnson; Cover Design—Marion Designs
Editors—Shonell Bacon, Candace K. Cottrell (Proofreader)

Special Thanks

First and foremost, all praises go to God for giving me this gift. If it weren't for his many blessings I wouldn't be able to entertain you.

Mom, thanks for always being down for me no matter what. We go through our ups and downs, but your love for me never changes . . . even when we're not speaking. If I never told you before I hope you know that I love you, and I hope I've made you proud.

Paul, you've been more of a father to me than my own dad has ever been. Thanks for stepping up to the plate, and looking out for me the way you do. I know I owe you tons of money, and I swear the first million I make I'll break you off. (LOL) Thanks for hearing me out when I needed to vent, and just being the coolest dude I know. You always keep it real, and I love you for that.

Tiffany, hurry up and make it to the WNBA so you can buy me a mansion. I hope you know that I'm proud of you, and I want you to finish school. You have what it takes to make it, and whatever you decide to do I'm behind you ten thousand percent.

Shanna, you're the sister I wish I had coming up. When we first met I didn't think we would click, but now we're like two peas in a pod. You've held me down for so long it's not even funny. You told me I would be a star, and hopefully I will be one real soon. You're the strongest sister I know, and no matter what happens in our lives just know that if you ever need me I'm there, no questions asked. Stay strong, something wonderful is coming your way. I can feel it.

Nakea, you don't know how glad I am to have met you. Even before I wrote an entire book and you only read one chapter you've been blowing my name up like I'm Star Jones or somebody. Good looking on everything you've ever done for me.

Mr. Ken Divine, it's been a while, but I'm happy to have ever been in your presence. Who knew that a Philly girl and a New Yorker could hook up and make it like we did? I had a ball doing *Stories To Excite You,* and I hope we can collaborate again soon. I'm missing you over here so holla when you can. I know you're busy being a star and all . . . LOL.

Aunt Karen, I did it! I know a lot of people thought I was B.S.ing when I said I was going to be a writer, but you never gave me any reason to doubt myself. The late night talks are greatly appreciated, and as dramatic as I can be, I like you because I can be real with you and not sugar coat how I really feel about something. I know sometimes you feel like the world is crumbling around you, but you always bounce back. That's how us Forrest women do. Your blessings are coming, and I'm sure you know it. I'll meet you around My Way's for a drink or two, and we'll reminisce like always. Luv Ya! Oh, and don't tell Sandy, but you've always been my favorite . . . (smile)

Sandy, you know I was just joking girl! Thanks for looking out for me over the years and giving me room to express myself. When I had nowhere to go you gave me a roof, and that says a lot. Things are going to work out for you, too. I know sometimes you feel like you're taken advantage of, but that's just you being kind hearted. You know what to do and you know when to say no so relax, and breath easy. Life is meant to be enjoyed so do just that.

Tisha and Shar, y'all get much love from here till eternity.

Shar, you keep me laughing all the time and I swear I be getting in trouble at work, but you make it worthwhile. Stay cool baby girl, you always got my back regardless. Good looking out. Tisha, you and me grew up more like sisters than cousins. You always have my back too, and believe me when I tell you I appreciate it. People be hatin' on me, but you and Shar always put them right in their place. Much love y'all, and I'll holla at y'all in book three.

Belinda and Tony, the book is done, finally. Both of you kept me motivated, and helped me get my book done sooner than I expected. Thanks for the ideas and critiques, and the strength to just get it finished. Belinda, you told me my books would be in the stores one day, and here I am with book number two. Thanks to both of you for the prayers, and just putting up with my crazy behind.

Mark Anthony, thanks for the opportunity, sweetie. Working with you has been the most pleasant book publishing experience I've ever had. It didn't matter whether I called you a million times with a million questions you made sure I was straight and that everything was in order. Thanks for letting me express myself, and I look forward to working with you on the next book. If I haven't told you yet, you the man, Mark! Thanks for everything.

If I left anyone out, believe me it wasn't intentional. I have love for everyone that has mad love for me, and don't be surprised to see your name in the next book's dedication.

In the Beginning . . .

Table For Three

Imagine that, imagine that, imagine that, imagine . . .

At 5'2", 136 pounds, dark chocolate skin, and almond eyes, sexy Monica is standing over me topless, in a red thong, and giving me one hell of a show. My girl is popping it like she's trying to get rent money and only has two days left to scrape it up. You would think there's a pole in the center of the bed the way she's rotating and grinding her body to the beat of the music.

My eyes are fixed on hers as she does a sensual butterfly all the way down until the lips of her tunnel kiss my stomach, leaving a wet spot where they landed. She bends over and a tattoo spelling her name in neat cursive peeks out over the band of her thong. She takes her right nipple into her mouth and caresses the other as she continues to move to the beat of the music. Her body seems to shimmer as light from outside lands on her skin.

Stepping off the bed, she bends over to remove her thong, afterwards hooking it onto my foot. A dildo magically appears as she crawls toward me. My legs spread invitingly when her lips make contact with the space behind my right knee. I hear R. Kelly hyping it up with the guitar, making the love of my life sweat just a little.

Well, the second love of my life. While I'm laying here, legs spread eagle and playing with my clit, I can't even get into it because I know I should be at home with my husband and two kids. I could just get up and go, but I don't feel like the drama and tears I have to see every time I'm ready to leave. I know in my heart that I have no damn business being here in the first place, but I was thinking with my pussy in anticipation of all the wonderful orgasms I would have. Shit at home died down a long time ago, but it wasn't until I found myself lying here looking up at another woman's breasts did the guilt set in.

It wasn't supposed to be like this. I knew I should be at home making love to my husband, but he wasn't producing multiple orgasms like Monica. She does things with her tongue no one has written about yet. She has ways of making me explode that my husband has no idea on how to find that spot, and I can forget about him lasting all night. The five minutes he gives me I can do myself. I need satisfaction that my own hands don't produce, and Monica gives me what I need without any questions.

I don't want to have to tell my partner what I want. After all these years, he should already know what makes me cum. If you're going to hit it from the back, put a finger in my asshole or leave a handprint on my ass cheek. Take it with one of my legs on your shoulder while you use your thumb to play with my clit. While I'm riding, take both of my nipples into your mouth at the same time. Do something besides pound me all hard for five minutes then roll over and fall asleep.

Then, if that wasn't enough, this fool wanted to invite company into our bed. And that's why I'm in this mess now.

It all started about two months before the twins' fourth birthday. It had already been eight months since my husband and I had so much as fondled each other, let alone had any actual sexual contact. He had been on my last nerve about having a threesome with some hoochie he'd met, and I was about tired of hearing it. All I got was five minutes. What was he gonna do? Break it down to two and a half minutes between the both of us? He must have been suffering from too much radiation from sitting up in that news station all day or something. And what the hell was this girl and I supposed to do? She could munch all the carpet she wanted to, but I DON'T GET DOWN LIKE THAT!!!

Back in the day, my husband and I made love constantly. It was nothing to be bent over the kitchen counter getting served from behind. He would be stroking me from the back with one finger playing with my clit and the other in my asshole, while kissing my neck and talking dirty to me all at the same time. I would ride him in the dining room chair until my legs hurt, and he would then pick me up and lay me on the table, devouring me from feet to head, and not necessarily in that order. He liked for me to hold my lips open so my clit stood right out as he simultaneously sucked on it and fingered me with three fingers the way I liked it.

All of that stopped for one reason or another, and I didn't feel like him or this girl he was trying to sell me on. It got to the point where this fool started leaving notes around the house, practically begging me to jump on board. One night he tried to show me a picture of the girl, and I just snapped. What part of "no" didn't he understand, the "n" or the "o"?

"Babe, just hear me out," he said, pleading on his knees at my side of the bed. "You won't even listen to what I have to say."

I remembered the days when he would be on his knees on my side of the bed, only my legs would be thrown over his shoulders as his lips and tongue would have me squirming and begging for mercy. But right then, the sight of him was contributing to my already pounding headache.

"James, I done told you fifty thousand damn times that I'm not doing it, so why do you keep asking me?"

He didn't even realize that I was ready to bust him in the head with the alarm clock. Why wouldn't he just go to sleep?

"Because you're not keeping an open mind."

"Would you want me to bring another dick into the bedroom?" I asked.

He looked at me like I was crazy and got up to go lay on his side of the bed.

That shut his ass right up, if only for a second. I was so damn tired of hearing about this Monica chick, I was ready to just go ahead and get it over with. This entire scenario was making me sick to my stomach. What his dumb ass didn't realize is I might have went along with it just to please him, but I'd be damned if I would be pressured into doing anything I wasn't down for.

"So, is doing it in the bedroom the problem?" he asked in a desperate voice.

"What? Didn't I just tell you I didn't want to talk about it?"

"I'm just saying that if your concern is bringing her into our home I could easily get us a room over at the Hyatt or the Marriott."

"James, how do you even know this girl? What kind of shit are y'all into over at T.U.N.N.?"

I'm guessing this fool couldn't see the big ass pile of salt on my shoulders. If we were in a cartoon, steam would've been coming out of my ears at that point.

"My buddy Damon hooked it up for me. It's his wife's sister or something like that. They do it all the time."

That only made me wonder what kind of freaky shit her

family was into. I don't know too many people just putting their own flesh and blood out there like that.

"What do you know about her, James? This chick could be HIV positive for all we know. There is no cure for that!"

"We would all be using protection," he said as if he was offended. Shit, I'm offended he won't let it go.

"Will she be putting a condom around her mouth?" I asked. "Semen and saliva can carry the same shit."

"Here you go taking the conversation to another level. Why can't you just relax and enjoy life for once? It's only this one time."

"What I'm about to do is enjoy this six hours of sleep. Goodnight!" And with that, I turned my behind over and went to sleep.

Of course it wasn't over. When I woke up, James was in the shower. As much as I hated to go in the bathroom while he was in there, I figured if I could at least brush my teeth, I could shower real quick and be out the house before he had a chance to come at me with some bullshit. I was hoping he wouldn't bring this Monica shit up at 6:37 in the morning because I would hurt him.

By the time I was done brushing my teeth and cleansing my face, James was stepping out of the shower. Through the mirror I peeked at his toned body, and semi-erect penis. At the age of thirty-two, standing at least six feet three inches, he still had the body of a college football player. He's definitely well endowed, but what difference did it make if he was only good for five minutes? He caught my eye as he was drying off and a sly smile spread across his face as he covered his midsection with the towel and went into the bedroom. I hopped in the shower and lingered a little longer because it was his morning to get the kids ready.

When I stepped out of the streaming water and into our

room, I could still smell his Cool Water cologne. That made me wet instantly, but he'd never know. I'd just as soon please myself than waste my shower on a few minutes with him. After putting my outfit together and plugging in the electric curling iron, I was finally able to sit on the bed and moisturize my skin. Out of the corner of my eye I noticed a single yellow rose on my pillow and a piece of heart-shaped chocolate with "I Love You" printed on the foil resting next to it. I smiled, but continued to rub my Happy by Clinque body lotion into my skin.

I loved my husband, and maybe we could talk about this entire threesome thing later.

Surprisingly he had nothing to say at breakfast. He smiled a lot, and that just pissed me off. Not that I had any conversation for him, but his being quiet made me nervous. At least if he was talking I'd know how to vibe off him. He just sat there smiling the entire time, and that just made me suspicious.

When I started gathering my stuff up to leave for work, he already had my briefcase and files along with my lunch stacked all nice and neat in the passenger seat of my 2003 Blazer. I got a kiss on the cheek, and he even offered to take the kids to childcare for me. Something was definitely up, and I wasn't at work for five minutes before I figured it out. I was looking through the files that I was supposed to be working on over the weekend when a hot pink folder that I don't remember having before caught my eye. When I opened it, a 5x7 photo of Monica was pasted to the left, and a three-page printout about her was on the opposite side. I was too shocked to be offended.

The pages included her date of birth, zodiac sign, likes and dislikes, a copy of her dental records, last HIV test results, and the results of her gynecologist exam, which I was glad to see were all negative. Her address and phone number were also included, along with directions on how to get to her house from my job off Map Quest. I had to laugh to keep from being pissed because I was sure my husband was going crazy.

If that wasn't enough, further inspection produced a key card from the Hyatt and an invite to meet him and Monica at the hotel restaurant for dinner. A note, handwritten by James, said the kids would be at his mother's house, and I should be at the hotel by seven. I put everything back in the folder, and went to my first meeting of the day. I didn't even want to think about that right now, and I had a few choice words for James later on.

When I returned to my office for lunch, I opened my door to at least three hundred yellow tulips crowding my space. On my desk sat a bouquet of tulips and white roses mixed in a beautiful Waterford crystal vase. My secretary informed me that they were delivered only ten minutes before I got there, and the card could be found next to the vase on my desk. I was too overwhelmed to think clearly and mechanically walked over to my desk to retrieve the card. It was in a cute yellow and white envelope to match the flowers, and was written with a gold pen. It read:

Jasmine,
You must know that you're the love of my life, and there is nothing in this world I wouldn't do to make you happy. This one time I want us to be happy together. Please reconsider . . .
                                        Love Forever,
                                        James

In that instant, I knew I would be at the hotel later. I figured this one time wouldn't kill me, and it might spice up our love life so that it would be like it used to. I hoped I wasn't making the biggest mistake of my life. After gathering my thoughts, I went on with the rest of my day, trying not to think about what I would be getting into later. I had a trial at two o'clock that I had to go to, and on my way there I mentally checked my schedule to make sure I would be out of the office by five and chillin' in the suite by five thirty. That way I could freshen up and put on something sexy for dinner.

I got out of court at four-thirty, having had my client's charges dismissed. That made me feel great, and I planned to take the next two days off to celebrate. When I got back to the office, my secretary was smiling at me and holding a vase with at least two-dozen powder pink roses accompanied by another card. She gave them to me and offered to open my office door because my arms were full. When I walked in I almost dropped the bouquet I was holding because I was totally surprised. As if all the yellow tulips weren't enough, my office was now crowded with just as many powder pink and white roses.

"Someone is either madly in love with you or is apologizing. Whatever it is, let me know your secret," my secretary said as if she really wanted an answer. I just turned to her with a smile on my face, stepped to the side, and closed my door. Me and her weren't cool like that, and then wasn't the time to start.

I sat the bouquet on my desk next to the one I received earlier. There was nowhere for me to sit, so I walked over to the picture window so I could gather my thoughts while I looked down onto the city from the twenty-third floor. The envelope holding the card smelled like Ralph by Ralph Lauren. That puzzled me for a second because I don't own that particular scent. When I opened the envelope and pulled the card out, little gold hearts and stars fell from it. The card was from Monica requesting my presence at the hotel later. I was flattered and speechless. Maybe she wasn't that bad after all.

Deciding to head on over, I left my secretary with directions to have all of the ladies in our department come get a bouquet to put on their desks. I wanted my office cleaned out except for the two bouquets on my desk. On my way to my Blazer I called to check up on the kids before stopping at Victoria's Secret for something sexy.

I decided on a cranberry spaghetti strap one-piece with matching thong. The gown was ankle length with thigh high splits on both sides, and the front dipped down all the way to my navel. The back opened to the middle of my back, showing off my curvaceous size ten, even after a set of twins. I purchased a bottle of Breathless perfume and a pair of sandals to match, and then made my way to the hotel.

When I got to the suite, pink and white rose petals decorated every inch of every room and floated in the Jacuzzi on top of rose-colored water. Yellow tulips sat in crystal vases around the living room and bedroom, and Maxwell's *Urban Hang Suite* played softly in the background from invisible surround sound speakers. A mixture of pink and white rose petals and yellow tulip petals covered the California king-sized bed. A bottle of Alize Red Passion sat in a crystal ice bucket accompanied by three long stemmed wine glasses on the end table closest to the bathroom door. On the other table was a glass bowl was filled with condoms of different textures and colors.

A note was tucked into the mirror in the bathroom with instructions to meet my dinner guests in the dining room at seven o'clock sharp. It was already six-thirty judging by the clock on the bedroom wall, so I stepped up the game as I showered, dressed, and did my hair in record time, all while not disturbing the romantic setup. I was walking into the dining room at five of seven. The waiter sat me in a cozy booth away from the other guests with a glass of Moet, a yellow tulip, and a powder pink rose courtesy of my husband and Monica. At exactly seven, my dinner guests walked in.

James was sharp, dressed in cream linen slacks with dark chocolate gator shoes that perfectly matched the button-down shirt with different shades of browns and tans swirled through it, compliments of Sean John fashions. His wedding band glistened and shined from the door, and the light bounced off it from all the way across the room. I could smell his Cool Water way before he reached the table.

Monica was equally impressive in a short, champagne-colored one piece that showed off perky breasts, and fell just above her knee. The bottom of her dress had that tattered look that people are wearing nowadays, and it accented her long, chocolate legs. Her toes peeked out of champagne stiletto sandals, and her soft, jet-black curls framed her face. Her make-up was flawless, and she smelled sweet.

I stood up as they made their way to the booth, and couldn't stop staring at them. When my husband and Monica reached the table, he gave me a soft, lingering kiss on my lips that made me wet instantly. He hadn't kissed me like that in months. Monica gave me a soft kiss on my cheek, and James made sure we were both seated before he took his seat.

Before we could start conversing, the waiter was at our table with appetizers. We were served stuffed mushrooms and Caesar salad with glasses of Moet to wash it down. I glanced over at my husband periodically and couldn't believe the thoughts I was having. For the first time in months, I wanted my husband the way a woman wants her man, and I couldn't wait to get upstairs.

"Did you get the roses I sent you?" Monica asked between small bites of the crab-stuffed mushroom she was eating. She had the cutest heart-shaped mouth that made you want to kiss her. Her tongue darted out every so often to the corners of her mouth to remove whatever food or drink was there. That turned me on and made me wonder how her tongue would feel on my skin.

"Yes, thank you. They were nice."

"Did you enjoy the tulips?" my husband asked, his eyes never leaving me. "I know yellow is your favorite color."

Tonight, he looked different, kind of like he was in love with me all over again. His eyes twinkled with mischief, and his lips begged for me to kiss him. I wanted to so badly.

"Yes baby, I did. Thank you."

"You're welcome, baby. How'd your day go?"

Me, Monica, and James made conversation over the smoked salmon, wild rice, and mixed vegetables we were served for dinner. Before dessert was served, James and I slow danced to "Reunion" by Maxwell as I watched Monica from the dance floor. She swayed from side to side in her seat, never taking her eyes off me. I don't know what she did when I wasn't facing her, but when I did she looked me right in the eye, her facial expressions telling me what I had to look forward to.

As we danced, my husband held me close, his mouth on my ear singing the words to the song. His warm hands felt good on my bare back as he made small circles, massaging me. I truly felt like this was indeed our reunion because it had been a long time since we'd been like this. I closed my eyes and tightened my arms around his neck, enjoying the feel of him in my arms and me in his.

Slices of double chocolate cake waited for us when we got back to the table. I couldn't touch mine because I was ready to go upstairs. James fed me and Monica his cake off the same fork, and that only made me more excited. I wanted to get this party started, but I went with the flow because I didn't know what they had planned.

"Are you ready for ecstasy, baby?" my husband asked me after we finished dessert. Instead of answering, I grabbed both of them by the hand and led them out of the dining room.

Anything Goes

Once we got into the elevator, James pulled us into a group hug, our heads resting on each of his shoulders. We looked at each other curiously, probably thinking about how far the other would go. Before I could react, Monica leaned over and kissed me, and it wasn't a peck on the lips, either. She slid her tongue into my mouth, allowing my taste buds to sample the chocolate cake left on it from dessert. Her lips felt soft as she sucked on my bottom lip, then my top, causing a tingling sensation to shoot down my back, straight to my toes, and finally resting warmly on my clitoris.

I could taste a hint of her cherry lip gloss when my tongue touched the corner of her mouth. A moan escaped my lips when her hand made contact with the left side of my neck, pulling my face closer to hers. I opened my eyes to look at her facial expressions while she kissed me, and to my surprise she was already watching me. I blushed, a little embarrassed at being caught, but she let me know it was cool by kissing my eyelids. She kissed the tip of my nose and went back to my lips while my husband made small circles on my back with his fingertips. Her kiss was slow and sensual, and thankfully not wet and sloppy like most men do. She allowed me to lead, then I allowed her to teach me what she knew.

My right hand found my husband's erect penis just as we were approaching the fourteenth floor. When I stepped back to adjust my hand around his shaft, the elevator suddenly stopped and the lights went out. We were all stuck on stupid for about thirty seconds. We were on our way to erotica beyond our wildest dreams and the damn elevator stopped. You talking about pissed! I finally got up the nerve to go through with this wild night and there I was stuck in a hot ass elevator. Oh, how I was *so* not in the mood for that.

"James, do something," I said while slightly hyperventilating. We were stuck between the thirteenth and fourteenth floors, and I wanted out.

"Baby, just calm down. I'll call the service desk to see what they can do."

While James was on the phone, I sat down in the corner to slow my heart rate and collect my thoughts. I didn't know how long we were going to be stuck, and that was not the place to pass out from lack of oxygen. I was hoping to still be in the mood when we got out, because at that moment I wanted to be off the elevator and in my bed.

Just as I leaned my head back against the wall, I felt a pair of warm hands parting my legs. I still heard James on the phone, and my body tensed up because I couldn't believe Monica was trying to sex me at a time like this. Cumming was the last thing on my mind, and I was almost certain everyone else felt the same way. Before I could protest, Monica had my thong pulled to the side, and her was tongue stroking my clit. Her tongue felt hot on my panic button, and the way she used her fingers made my knees touch the elevator walls instantly.

She took her time moving two fingers in and out of me

while she sucked, licked, kissed, and played havoc with my clit trapped between her lips. My body shook involuntarily because I was trying not to explode. I didn't want to moan aloud while James was on the phone, but it was killing me trying to hold it in. She held the lips of my cave open and her tongue snaked around inside me, my walls depositing my sweet honey on her tongue. For a second, it felt like we were the only two people trapped in that hot box.

"Okay ladies, the attendant said we'd only be in here for a—damn," when James hung up the phone and looked over at our silhouettes in the dark, he was speechless. I guess the sight of his wife being pleased by another woman shocked him.

His back was to us the entire time, so it had to have been a pleasant surprise to see Monica and me the way we were. James never could do more than one thing at a time, so it didn't surprise me that he didn't pay us any mind until he was done with his call.

He stood back and watched for a while, taking in the sights and sounds of what was happening. With the little bit of light coming from the call box, I could see James massaging his strength through his pants. He squatted down behind Monica, lifting her dress up over her hips, exposing her heart-shaped ass. My eyes had adjusted to the dark, and even though I couldn't clearly see what was happening, his outline said it all. Monica was in the doggy-style position with her head buried between my legs. James had inserted his fingers into her walls just as Monica did to me only moments earlier. I could see James maneuvering his body so that he could taste her. In the meantime, Monica was pulling another orgasm out of me.

She moaned against my clit from my husband pleasing her. The more James pushed and pulled on her, the more intense her pleasing me became. I scooted forward so that I could lay flat on the floor. Monica stood up and positioned herself over me. She pulled her French-cut panties to the side, and placed her pussy lips on my mouth. I just imitated what she did to me, switching from kissing and sucking her clit, and sticking my tongue inside her. James was inside of me, stretching my walls to fit him.

He stroked me slow, teasing me with just the head before sliding it all in. His thumb created friction on my clit and before we could stop it, I exploded on his length and Monica exploded in my mouth. We were about to switch positions when the lights came on and the elevator started moving. James pulled out of me still rock-hard, making it a little difficult to pull up the zipper on his pants.

When the elevator door opened, the attendant and the security guard were waiting on the other side. They tried to apologize, but we just rushed past them and scrambled down the hall to our suite so we could finish what we started. We didn't think about the fact that they could probably smell sex in the air, and I don't think we really cared.

Upon entry to the room, Monica went to run hot water into the Jacuzzi because the water that was in there got cold. I sat on the side of the bed, anxiety covering me like a blanket. I couldn't believe what I'd just done and what I was about to do. I was excited and scared at the same time. I was excited because I was finally letting go of my inhibitions and stepping outside the box, but scared because I didn't want to disappoint my husband.

I'll never do this again, I thought, but I did want him to enjoy this night of pleasure.

Monica came out of the bathroom in her bra and panties. I was hesitant about looking her in the eye because I knew my cheeks were red from blushing. We were all silent, not wanting to be the one to say something first. James changed the CD in the stereo to a slow-jams mix he put together. When R. Kelly started crooning, "Come to Daddy," Monica started doing an erotic dance in front of the full-length mirror. James leaned back on the dresser to watch the show, and I just sat there with a shocked expression on my face. She danced like she'd had ballet lessons, but with just enough eroticism to make you think she might have been wrapped around a pole in a strip club once or twice.

As she got closer to me, I scooted back on the bed to keep her at arm's length. What we did in the dark elevator was cool because I couldn't see it, but now we were in a well-lit room with my husband able to see everything. I wasn't sure if I wanted to go through with it, but when I looked over at James stroking his length and gazing at us I couldn't stop. Just the fact that he'd been hard for more than five minutes was amazing.

The look on my face screamed, "HELP" as I looked from James to Monica. Monica advanced toward me slowly, and James smiled as he watched us work. I was now up against the headboard with my legs up to my chest. When Monica reached me, she took my feet into her hands and started to massage them one at a time. I was as stiff as a virgin on her first night, and Monica did her thing to help me relax.

She took my toes into her mouth, one at a time. My moans escaped involuntarily. Her soft lips traveled up my thighs until they rested against my pelvis. Her tongue dipped in and out of my honey pot. She held my lips open with both hands, exposing my now wet pearl to my husband.

"James, can I taste it?" Monica asked my husband in a husky voice. I looked over at him to read his face. It showed nothing but excitement.

"Go ahead and make her cum," he responded in a deep, passionate voice. His hand moved at a slow, lazy pace up and down his erect shaft. A hint of pre-cum rested on the tip of his penis, and I motioned him over to the bed so I could taste it.

He disrobed on his way over, his body looking like he should be on the cover of *GQ* magazine. Monica had her full lips pressed against my clit, causing me to squirm and breathe heavily. James stood beside the bed with his chocolate penis standing straight out. I didn't hesitate to wrap my lips around him, taking as much in as I could without choking.

James fondled our breasts simultaneously while trying to maintain his balance as I gave him head. Monica held my legs up, and kept her face buried in my treasure chest. Our moans were bouncing off the walls, tuning out the music that was playing. If there were people in the suite next to us, I was sure they heard everything.

Monica moved back off the bed and pulled me with her. James lay down in the middle of the bed on his back, his erection pointing at the ceiling. I straddled his thickness like a pro, dipping all the way down until my clit touched his pelvis then coming back up until just the head was in. James leaned up on his elbows and took my nipples into his mouth one at a time. Monica had my ass cheeks spread so that her tongue could make acquaintance with my asshole. I was having orgasms back to back like I used to when me and James first met. I was damn near about to pass out from exploding so much.

We switched positions in order to relax a little more. Monica put on a strap-on vibrator with clitoral stimulators around the base. I looked at her like who did she think she was using that on. She took James's place in the center of the bed and motioned for me to get on top of her. I looked at her and my husband like they were crazy.

"James, I am not getting on her like that. She done . . ." the mood was changing quickly, and Monica was looking frustrated. Ask me did I give a damn. Some shit just ain't meant to be tried, and this was one of them.

"Baby, it's okay. It'll feel just like the real thing. Trust me on this one," James said to me in a calm soothing voice. I wasn't buying it.

"And what are you going to do with that?" I asked referring to his erect penis.

"You'll see, and you'll enjoy it. Just trust me."

He gave me a reassuring look as he led me to the bed. I closed my eyes and got on top of Monica, doing to her what I did to my husband. It was feeling good, and I really got into it. When I bent over to kiss Monica, I felt a warm liquid oozing down the crack of my ass. My husband held my back so that I couldn't move, and I could feel him inserting a finger into my forbidden place. I tensed up automatically, and he whispered to me to try to relax.

I don't do back shots, and my husband knew that. I wanted to get an attitude, but what they were doing felt good. I reminded myself that it was only one night, and I tried to relax myself so that my husband could join in the fun. I wondered how he was going to fit it in because he was definitely blessed in the dick department. He's long and thick, with a big mushroom-shaped head that I knew was way bigger than the hole he would try to get it into. It would be like trying to put a block into a round hole. A finger in the ass was one thing. He could do that all day, but ten inches in the ass was something to scream about.

"James, I don't think I'll be able to take it back there, baby," I whispered. "You're too big."

I was hoping he would have second thoughts when he heard how scared I was, but that wasn't the case.

"Jasmine, I won't hurt you, baby. I'll take my time, and I'm using this so you'll be okay." He held out a bottle of KY Warming Liquid for me to view.

"Won't it get too hot back there?"

"You'll be fine, just relax," Monica responded before taking my nipples into her mouth. A moan escaped from my lips, totally catching me off guard.

I tried to relax as James eased himself into my back door. Lord knows it was killing me, but I stuck in there. He slowly pushed the head in, which was the most painful part. It felt like he was ripping me a new ass hole, and tears gathered at the corners of my eyes, threatening to fall and land on Monica's forehead. Once he got in as much as he could comfortably, he began pleasing me with long slow strokes. In combination with Monica pushing and pulling on the bottom, I was going crazy from the new feelings I was having. When James pulled out, Monica pushed in, causing me to lose my breath on more than one occasion. James reached around my waist and teased my clit while Monica held my lips open for him. His other hand fondled my right nipple while Monica's mouth warmed the other one.

I didn't know whether I was coming or going. Some time during the mix, the pace quickened and we were going at it like animals. Monica sat on the lounge chair with vibrator in hand, watching me and James become one. He held me by my ankles, pushing my legs all the way back, my knees touching my ears easily. He was driving his penis deep in me with slow strokes, and I never wanted him to stop.

"I'm cumming, baby," I said to my husband between inhaling and exhaling. "Cum with me."

James slowed it down, and we looked each other as our orgasms played out. My legs wrapped around him tightly until our rapture subsided. Monica looked spent as she too was exploding along with us. James pulled out of me and rested with his head between my breasts while we caught our breath. The session we just had was the best thing since sliced bread.

"I'll meet y'all in the Jacuzzi," Monica replied as we reluctantly untangled ourselves from each other. At that moment, I wanted Monica to leave so James and I could enjoy our weekend alone, but I didn't want to be rude. I later found out that was mistake number one. The red light was practically blinking right in front of my face, but for reasons beyond even me, I went with the flow instead of stating my wishes. She served her purpose, and it was time for her ass to go.

We joined Monica in the Jacuzzi a little while later. James popped open one of the Alize bottles, and we sat back and chilled. *Friday After Next* was playing in the DVD player, but I paid it no mind. I wanted some more of my husband, but with Monica there, I knew it would be a group thing. We relaxed a little longer, and before the movie was over we scrubbed each other clean and dried ourselves off.

James had another movie playing in the room while we fell back on the huge bed. He told us of our plans for the next day. Monica would only be with us for tonight. After breakfast, she would be heading home, leaving me and James to enjoy the rest of our mini-vacation, which was cool with me because I was ready for her to leave anyway. I didn't see why she had to stay the entire night. I mean, he could have easily put her in a cab and sent her on her merry way. I started to suggest that to James, but I didn't want to spoil the mood. He also made mention of a shopping spree and a couple's spa treatment we would be attending at the hotel.

I half watched the movie, and half played back what went down earlier. Out of the corner of my eye, I took in Monica. She was definitely a cutie and I could see why James thought her to be the perfect candidate for our evening of adventure. She had skills and knew what she was doing, but I couldn't help but wonder how much it took for her to be here. Had she and James hooked up before? I tried not to entertain the thought, but it was bugging me. Then, on top of all that, I was wondering if I could maybe hook up with her on the ducky at a later date. She was phenomenal, and I wanted to see exactly what she could do. Maybe it was just the liquor talking, but I was definitely thinking about meeting up with her soon.

We gave each other full body massages, and orally pleased each other until we drifted off to sleep. The next morning we showered together and had breakfast over conversation of our activities the previous evening. When James got up to use the restroom, Monica just kind of stared at me. I wanted to ask her if I had a boogey in my nose or something. For some reason I felt a little uncomfortable.

"So, Jasmine, did you enjoy yourself last night?" she asked as if she really wanted to know. I answered after watching her tie the stem of a cherry into a knot with her tongue.

"Yeah, it was different. I had fun," I said nonchalantly. I did not want to have this conversation with her. I was still thinking about having her one on one, but I wouldn't dare approach the subject.

"Well, if you want us to hook up under more private circumstances, you know how to contact me."

"I'll do that."

Just then, James joined us at the table. He thanked Monica for a wonderful evening, and put her in a cab to go home. I saw the envelope he slipped her, but decided not to comment on it. We went back to our suite to change, and then we went on the shopping spree. We only had three hours to shop because James scheduled our spa time for early afternoon.

We made it back to the hotel with ten minutes to spare before we had to go and get pampered. Instead of shopping, we ended up going to a miniature golf course. We had a ball as we missed hole after hole because neither of us could hit the ball straight. After that we had lunch at the Hibachi, a five-star Asian bar located on Delaware Avenue. It felt like we were dating again and I didn't want the day to end. I did pick up a pair of sexy stiletto sandals from Charles David before we went back. I had a thong to match them perfectly, and that's all I planed to wear with them later that night.

All too soon our weekend was over and it was time to go back to work. We had a good time just hanging out and being stress-free, and we got into some hellified sex sessions that left me speechless and smiling every time. No more of the five-minute poundings going on. We made love for hours. Sometimes it was slow, sometimes it was heart-pounding fast, but it was more than five minutes, and that's what mattered. We took pictures on the strip and some nude ones in the room. We also climbed into the big champagne glass shaped Jacuzzi and had our picture taken, and once the picture guy was gone, we got it on something fierce, splashing bubbles all over the place.

Before we left I made sure everything was packed and we weren't forgetting anything. I sat on the lounge chair to catch my breath and enjoy the room for a second longer. James was in the restroom making sure he packed all of our toiletries. When he came back in the room, he kneeled in front of me and put his head in my lap.

"Jasmine, I am so happy you are my wife. This weekend was wonderful, and I appreciate you going through with our plans. You have made me very happy," James said while rubbing the backs of my legs.

"I'm glad you enjoyed yourself. We needed to get away for a second," I responded while fondling the wavy texture of his hair.

Instead of responding, he reached under my skirt and pulled my panties to the side. I couldn't protest because he was already tasting me. We went at it for another hour, and were late checking out. We had to pay a fee, but it was well worth it.

Mistake Number One

Once James and I got home, things were better than ever. For the first time in months, we made love on a daily basis, and sometimes three or four times a day. In the past two months, we've met up for quick sessions during lunch, and we'd sneak off into the garage late at night while the kids were sleeping to add a little spice to our lovemaking. James sent me tulips at least twice a week, and we made it a must-do to have dinner out on Saturday nights just so we could have our time together. We made acquaintance with the kitchen table on more occasions than I can remember, and life was good.

I didn't think much about Monica, and for me that night was a distant memory—a thing we never spoke about once we left the hotel. I never let on to how much I really enjoyed myself and that I was seriously contemplating doing it again. Monica made my skin feel like it was on fire. I love a nice stiff one, but her soft lips could be a wonderful replacement.

The only thing that kept me from going through with it was my job. I didn't want anyone at the firm thinking I was a "swinger" or anything like that, and a scandal of that caliber could ruin everything James and I worked so hard for. We had our children to think about, and the high-priced vehicles that we were pushing around town. We were used to living ghetto fabulous, and I couldn't see anything that petty taking it all away, no matter how wet my pussy got thinking about her.

I pushed that thought out of my head almost as soon as I thought of it and tried to refocus on my most troublesome client, Bryan Campbell. He was a petty thief who just couldn't seem to stay clean. I personally think he likes jail more than he likes his freedom. He told me once that at least in the "pen" he's guaranteed three free meals a day, and that there are more drugs on the inside than in his neighborhood.

It's sad because he could make some woman a good husband. The drugs have him tore down, but you can tell that if he cleaned himself up he could be fly. I was working his case because the last number he pulled landed him almost six years. He and his cronies decided they wanted to be like the girls in *Set It Off* and rob a bank. Never mind they ain't have any guns. Well, he didn't. This fool was holding the guard hostage with a sausage in his pocket. I wanted to bust him in his head myself.

One of the guys he was with shot the guard in the chest, and everyone got away but him. He was sitting in jail because he didn't want to tell who did what, and on top of that, he was a repeat offender, so the judge just threw a stack of books at him. I wanted to leave him in there for being stupid, but you know you have to work each case to the best of your ability.

So I was in my office trying to wrap up my long, tiring day when my secretary buzzed me to let me know I had a delivery. I didn't think anything of it as I circled around my desk to pick up what I assumed to be a package. When I opened my office door, a beautiful bouquet of powder pink roses was waiting for me.

Speaking of the devil, I thought to myself.

I thanked my secretary and picked up the bouquet to take it to my office. Before I could close the door, my secretary called out to me.

"Mrs. Cinque, I have to say I admire you," she commented with a straight face. I was puzzled as to what brought that about.

"Why is that?"

"Because you bust your behind around here day in and day out, and to me it seems to go unnoticed. Then your husband does little things like send flowers to let you know he's thinking about you, and it all seems to be okay. My son's father would never do that."

I didn't know what to say, and my face must have said it all. The funny thing is she's been my secretary for the past two years and I can't even think of her name at this moment. I wanted to say something positive, but my mind drew a blank. I could smell Monica's perfume coming from the card in the bouquet, and I wanted to hurry and open it.

"You'll know when you've found the right one. Believe me," and with that said I closed my door and went to inspect my card.

Monica has beautiful, curvy handwriting that matches her perfectly. The way you write says a lot about you, and her script is just as sassy as she. She wrote a short paragraph inviting me to have dinner with her in her home, WITHOUT MY HUSBAND. She said that the night we spent together had been on her mind, and she wanted to show me pleasures I could only dream about. I was shocked, but pleased at the same time. That night we shared was nice, but I really wanted her to leave because my husband did things to me he hadn't done in a good long while, but what she did was hardly over-looked. The girl had skills; I had to give it her.

Now my dilemma was this: we shared that one night on some threesome type stuff, but wouldn't me and her one-on-one make me bisexual? I mean, lets be real. The first time was just experimentation, the second time is just being greedy, and any time after that its curtains. Don't get me wrong, I'm very comfortable with my sexuality, but Monica was the bomb with a capital B. If she could make me feel like I felt that night, I thought I may just have to see her again.

At the end of the note she included her address and phone number, and asked that I confirm our meeting by five-thirty this evening. I looked at my watch and it was al-ready 5:20. I didn't know what to do, but curiosity got the best of me, and I decided to go for it. We were only having dinner, but my walls were already contracting. Monica can turn you into Spider Woman in no time, and I was ready to go there. Now, what do I tell James?

Before I had my story together, I was already dialing the number to the studio, and hoping I could come up with something by the time he answered the phone. I already de-cided to call my brother so that he could watch the kids until James got home, and I promised myself that I would not stay over there too late. As soon as I exploded, I would leave.

"Thank you for calling The Urban News Network. This is Cindy, how may I direct your call?"

Cindy is the overly polite receptionist over at the station. If it weren't for her looking to be well past a hundred years old, it would be cool. Her voice and her appearance clashed like a fat girl in a polka dot dress. Wasn't anything sexy about it.

"Hi Cindy, can you connect me to James, please?"

"Sure, Mrs. Cinque. Hold for a second." She put me on

hold and Anita Baker crooning about being in sweet love flowed through my receiver. I felt bad for a second because I loved James, and even though Monica is the same sex as me, it was still cheating. I started to back out and just go make love to him instead until he answered the phone.

"Thanks for calling The Urban News Network, who am I speaking with?" James answered with his deep voice. It sounded like things were a little hectic over there, and he was a little agitated.

"Hey, sweetheart. How's your day going?"

"Hey, baby. I was just about to call you. Our system shut down unexpectedly and we've been trying to get it together for the past hour. I might be here all night."

"Baby, just relax. You're the best they have over there, and whatever the problem is, you can fix it. That's why you're the Director of Engineering."

"Thanks babe, but I know we had plans to dip off later, and I don't want to disappoint you."

"Sweetie, it's okay. I was calling to tell you I would be running late because I'm trying to finish up with the paperwork from the Campbell case, and Trish just made partner, so we were going to get a few drinks afterwards to celebrate." I felt like shit. Those lies rolled off too easily. Well, they weren't total lies. Trish did make partner, but that was like last week and technically I was working on a case, but I was putting it to the side to go bump coochies with Monica. If James even thought I was still seeing Monica, he'd probably die. I know I would be pissed if he were stepping out.

"Tell Trish I said congrats. I'm sorry about tonight, and I'll make it up to you tomorrow, okay?"

"Okay, baby. Don't stress too much. It'll be fine."

"I know, boo, I know. I love you. Be safe."

"I will, and I love you too. Talk to you later."

We blew each other a kiss then hung up. I called Monica

next to confirm, and she told me that dinner was almost done, and that I could come on through. I straightened up my desk and put everything in order so that I could bust it out when I came in tomorrow morning. I hate clutter, and never left my desk a mess. Afterwards, I freshened up in my private bathroom and made my way down to Monica's to enjoy dinner . . . and whatever dessert came with it.

I was having all kinds of doubts on my drive over to Monica's house. I knew we would sleep together; that went without saying. My only problem was if James ever found out there would be some serious explaining to do. He would have questions, and I knew I couldn't possibly give him an honest answer. How do you tell your husband his sex is the bomb, but you prefer the feel of another woman's lips to his? That wouldn't go over too nicely.

When I pulled up to her house I wasn't the least bit surprised. She lived in a cute, two-story, Victorian-style home that sat way back off the street. Her house had a beautiful wrap-around porch set off by a well-manicured lawn. There was a wooden swing off to the left that was perfect for cool summer nights. Her windows sported pastel pink shutters to match the trim on her white house. She had several rose bushes sprinkled around her yard, and her address hung from a powder pink mailbox on a black address hanger. It was written in script with little roses around the border. Monica definitely loved pink flowers.

By the time I parked my car and began to walk up the path to her door, she was already standing there. Monica was a lot shorter than I remembered. A cute little petite something. She had on a halter dress that stopped just under her ass and showed off her perfect legs. Her hair was done in one of those spiky styles like Halle Berry would wear that showed more of her pretty face and bright eyes.

She greeted me with a tight hug like she really missed me,

and invited me into her home. The inside was just as breath-taking. She had a sunken living room decorated in pastel yellows, pinks, and blues. Her walls had splashes of all three colors to match the designs in her furniture. The fireplace was to die for, and I could almost picture us lying in front of it on a cold winter night touching and tasting each other.

There was a spiral staircase with steps made of clear marble with rose petals embedded in them. The railing was gold plated with a vine design wrapped around it with crystal roses appearing to bud from it. She had pictures of couples making love in various positions on top of pink rose petals with gold leaves. The flowers really stood out because the couples were sketched in black and white. It wasn't until I took a closer look that I realized that Monica was the woman in the pictures. That left me speechless.

Her dining room was nothing but candlelight. An intimate placement for two was set on her pure ivory dining table. Candles burned in ivory candleholders, and silk dinner napkins sat beside patterned china. Lasagna and buttered crescent rolls shaped like hearts were presented in crystal dishes. A bottle of Alize Red Passion and two slightly chilled crystal flutes topped off the décor. I was still speechless.

Her kitchen housed every kitchen gadget you could think of. Her Sub Zero refrigerator encased in chrome was absolutely beautiful. Pink and white found its home here also in the shape of window curtains, pot holders, and countertops. A little dinette set made of wood took up space in one corner of her huge kitchen. I thought my house was saying something until I walked up in there.

Through the back door I could see her swimming pool, and I had to get a closer look. When I looked in, a portrait of Monica in a pink teddy could be seen painted on the bottom. I wanted to hate, but I was living good so there was no reason to complain. I just wanted to know what she did for a living to be able to afford all of this. I wanted to see the up-stairs, but she suggested we eat dinner before it got cold. I mean, hell, we would be up there later anyway.

We had polite conversation while we enjoyed our meal. I was a little nervous and resisted the urge to jet several times. I felt so bad about being there while James was stressing at work, and the fact that I lied to him about where I was made me feel even worse. Monica kind of picked up on my mood and suggested we continue our conversation on the couch. I'm sure she was thinking it was something she did, but that was far from the case.

Once we got comfortable on her sofa, we resumed con-versation while she rubbed my feet. It felt so good I could hardly talk. Before I knew it, my head was resting on the arm of the sofa and I was almost asleep. For a second I thought I was at home. I felt James massaging my feet turn into him moving his soft hands up my leg. Then I'm like *How did his hands get so soft all of a sudden?* When I opened my eyes, Monica's hands were high on my thighs, my prize not far away. Surprisingly, I didn't flinch or pull back. I almost wanted her to hurry up because I knew it was going to be good.

She stood up, I assumed, to take her clothes off. She walked toward the stairs, leaving pieces of clothing along the way. It wasn't a lot because she didn't have much on to begin with. By the time she got to the third step, she was standing in noth-ing but a thong, and I was like *damn*. She looked even better than the last time. Her chocolate skin made you want to kiss her all over, and her nipples were just a shade darker than the rest of her body, putting you in mind of a Hershey's kiss. I was hesitant at first, but I followed her up the stairs and into the master bedroom.

Totally different from the downstairs, her bedroom was

decked out in neutral colors. Dark browns, honey, tan, hunter green, and maroon made this room look very sexy. Her sleigh bed sat up off the floor, and you had to walk up about four steps to climb into it. The furnishings were made out of heavy cherry wood that she has definitely paid some money for. I stood just inside the doorway, taking it all in.

Monica turned on the stereo, and I felt like I was listening to a late night smooth grooves session on the radio. She walked over to me and took my hand, leading me to the steps that led up to her bed. No words were needed as she slowly undressed me, kissing the body parts she revealed on the way down. My head was screaming, "get the hell out of here", but the rest of my body was whispering, "girl, you about to explode, so chill."

She walked me up to her bed and told me to lay flat on my stomach. I did what I was told and closed my eyes, listening to the melody in the background. She straddled me, her warmth and wetness seeping into my pores, and causing a puddle of my own nectar to form under me. The oil she poured onto my back was cool on my already hot skin, but her hands warmed it up in no time. The room smelled like chocolate instantly. Monica was good at what she did, causing all of the tension in my body to leave almost instantly. James became a distant memory as I moaned under the hands of this woman.

She kissed the center of my back as she massaged me, her juice caressing my skin from her pressing her clit against me. She ran her hands down between my thighs, her thumb entering my tunnel then pulling out quickly. She traced the outside of my lips with her well-oiled finger, and I moaned like she done put something in me. I didn't even remember turning over, but Monica was kneeling on my right side massaging the front of me, her tongue feeling hot on my sensitive nipples. I tried to stay cool, but my back arched to meet her lips. I was about to cum, and we hadn't done anything yet.

Monica tied a silk scarf around both of my wrists and attached both arms to the headboard. Now, I was like *hold the hell up*. I don't even let James tie me down, but Monica didn't give me time to protest. She was between my legs and on my clit before I could say anything. It was a good thing my hands were tied because otherwise they would have been holding her head while I glazed her face completely.

She took her time "inspecting" me. Monica held both lips open, leaving room for her tongue to explore all of me. My legs were spread into a perfect V while she sucked and licked on me. She put her tongue so far up in me you couldn't have told me she didn't touch my cervix. I moaned like crazy and tried to catch my breath because she was pulling orgasms out of me left and right.

I felt something cold slide inside of me, and almost lost it completely. On the side of the bed I noticed amongst the bottles of oils and body butters sat two long and thick dildos made of ice. She must have had three, because one was inside of me driving me crazy. I was exploding all over it, almost ashamed because I was messing up her bedspread. She sucked on my clit and worked the ice in and out of me until there was only a small piece left. Silly me thought she would just toss it out. Monica put the ice in her mouth and pushed it into my cave using her tongue. She would push it up and suck it out, causing a whole 'nother explosion until it was gone.

The fact that my thighs had her in a serious headlock didn't seem to bother her or mess up her rhythm. She continued to push and pull on my clit until I was screaming for mercy, opening my legs wide so she could move her head. She leaned up to look at me, her wild hairstyle still in place. She

licked my essence off her lips seductively while her middle
and forefinger still played around my insides. My walls were
gripping her like she had a penis and soon I found myself
exploding again.

"Now, I'm going to let you go," Monica said in a soft sexy
voice, "but only if you're ready to go there."

"Go where?" I asked already knowing the answer. She just
gave me one of those "stop playing with me" looks before
leaning over to the table next to the bed.

"If you don't know I guess I need to use another one of
these," she said referring to the ice shaped penises she had
sitting on the side. I knew for sure I couldn't take any more
of that.

"No, I got you. You can untie me now."

She motioned for me to scoot down to the middle of the
bed. I did as I was told with my arms still stretched out. She
stood over me with her legs on either side of my head. Slowly
she bent her knees until her lips rested on mine. My tongue
found her opening instantly. She untied one hand and undid
the other one once I captured her clit between my lips. I could
see Monica's hands on the wall helping her to keep her balance over top of me.

I was barely able to reach the table, but managed to snag
one of the ice pieces without missing a beat. I continued to
stimulate her clit while teasing her with the ice just at the
opening of her tunnel. She moaned in appreciation as I
teased her with just the head before sliding it all in. I positioned the ice-cold sculpture on my chin and she rode my
face like she was riding a real dick with me capturing her clit
in my mouth when she came down, and her pulling it out on
the way up. The ice melted quickly from her warmth. Her
juices flowed effortlessly. I stuck my index finger in her asshole for good measure, and my girl went wild.

She stood up off my face and placed herself softly on my

stomach, her explosion running down my sides and forming puddles on both sides of me. She rotated on me with her eyes closed, moaning until it was over. I rubbed her clit with my thumb until her shaking subsided and she was able to open her eyes and look at me. I blushed a little at what just went down, partly because I didn't think I had it in me to please another woman. The bullshit orgies I had in college never got this intense, and I never had to use so much of my imagination. I never wanted to. I was always on the receiving end and never had to put much into a performance, so this was something new.

Don't ask what made me do it, but for some reason I looked across the room toward the dresser and the clock caught my eye. I thought my eyes were playing tricks on me until I sat up in the bed.

"Does that clock say ten-thirty?" I needed her to tell me because I didn't want to believe it.

"Yes. Why, are you in a rush?"

"Hell yeah! I didn't tell James I would be out this long. He's going to kill me."

"It's still early. Don't you want to finish up in the shower? I have some treats in there waiting, and . . ."

"Did I not just tell you I had to roll? I ain't got no business being here in the first place. My husband is going to kill me."

In the midst of me running around the room trying to find the damn light switch and a washrag, I thought I heard Monica sniffling. In the middle of my panic performance, I stopped to look at her. She was curled up in the middle of the bed crying. Even though the room was semi-dark, I could see her shoulders move up and down with every sob. I started to just leave her like that, but my heart wouldn't let me do it. I guess, for some odd reason, I cared about her. Dropping my head in defeat, I walked over to the bed to see what was wrong with her.

"Monica," I called out to her softly as I made my way up the steps to her bed, "sweetie, what's wrong?" I sat and listened to her, but on the real I wanted her to hurry the hell up. I had to get to the west side in twenty-three minutes and four seconds.

"Nothing . . . I don't want you to go."

"I have to go sweetie, but I'm sure there will be other times."

"You promise?" she asked as she sat up on the bed and wiped her nose with the sheet.

"I promise, but right now I need to get washed so I can go home and tend to my family. Can you help me do that?" I asked, hoping my gentleness would get her ass out the bed and some light in this room.

She got out of the bed looking like a helpless little girl, and I tried not to give a damn. I just wanted to hurry up and get home. She finally turned the light on and allowed me to see what was what. While she ran the shower, I gathered my clothes from the floor and tried to press the wrinkles out the best I could with my hands.

Without saying anything, she pulled me into the bathroom and into the shower, washing me quickly but thoroughly. She tried to go down on me in the shower, but I gently reminded her I didn't have time. Once we were done, she dried me off and gave me a cotton sweat suit she'd purchased for me to put on along with a new pair of sneakers to match. She said she figured I would need them since my clothes were a mess now.

I thanked her as I got dressed in record time. I practically ran to the door after I put my belongings into the bag my new outfit came in, but for some reason I couldn't find my panties. I told her if she found them to hold them for me, and I rolled out. When I got in my car, I could see Monica standing in the window waiting for me to pull off. I got

home before James, and was in the bed a half hour before
he came in. I tried to play like I was just waking up when he
came into the room.

"Hey babe," he said to me after kissing my cheek, "how
was the celebration?"

"It was cool. I only had a few wine coolers then I came on
home," I lied to my husband with a straight face. I felt horrible because he looked like he'd had a rough day at work
while I was out busting nuts with Monica across town.

"That's good, baby. Can we talk in the morning? Right
now I need to close my eyes for a second and get some
sleep."

I turned over on my side so he could lie in my arms. He
was asleep almost instantly. I was awake thinking about what
happened with Monica for hours. The sex was off the chain,
but the entire scene at the end threw me off completely. I
didn't really know what to make of it, but decided it wasn't
worth the effort as I finally drifted off to sleep.

No More, No Less

For the next two months, I tried to avoid Monica like fat girls should avoid horizontal stripes and attend Weight Watchers meetings. I felt absolutely horrible about how things went down on that night, and even worse when James woke up the next morning wanting to make love. I felt like he was getting sloppy seconds, and the night before did indeed get sloppy. The entire time James was in me I kept thinking about the ice sculptures and Monica's warm hands. A few times I almost slipped up and called her name out when James thought he was making me cum. I mean, I came, but it was because I was thinking about Monica's tongue roaming all over me. Not because he was banging my back out.

I received flowers and 'Thinking of You" cards constantly from Monica and James, and it began to get a bit overwhelming. James would just pop up at the office unexpectedly and I would have to hide the numerous cards Monica sent me and make up excuses as to where I was getting all the roses from. He hinted that maybe he knew Monica was sending them to me, but he never came right out and said it. The two of them competing for my time was exhausting, and I needed to get away from both of them for a while. I was seriously considering packing up me and my kid's stuff and going to Mexico. The two of them together were nerve-racking.

One day at the office, Monica and James must have been playing tag-team on the phones because no soon as I hung up from one the other would call, and vice versa. I'm like, *What the hell? I'm trying to get some work done, and these two are acting like fools.* It was like they knew what was up, and were trying to outdo each other. But in actuality, all they were doing was giving me a damn headache. During one conversation with Monica, shit got tense real quick and I had to hang up on her.

"Why don't you ever tell me you love me back? I show affection toward you twenty-four seven, even when you're at home playing house with James and the crew. Are you saying you don't care about me?" Monica asked like she honestly expected me to give her an answer.

Monica had been crying in my ear for the past twenty minutes about my so-called "lack of affection." How much affection did she want? I go down on her more than I do the person I'm married to. She doesn't even have to ask for it; it's a given. James had to damn near beg me to suck his dick, and even then it's only until he gets it up enough to slide it in me.

"Monica, we have been over this so many times already. I don't love you, I'm not in love with you, and *James and the crew* are my family. They come first, and you act like you don't know that," I said after taking a deep breath. I hated when she got like that.

"That's stuff I already know, but . . ."

"Then why do you keep asking me do I love you if you already know the answer?"

"Because I know you have to care about me a little bit or else you wouldn't keep coming here," she said through her tears. I hated to hear her cry, and I was trying my best to console her so that I could get off the phone. I had a court date in a half hour, and I did not have time to be dealing with this emotional-ass Virgo.

"Monica, look," I said through clenched teeth as calmly as possible, "I care about you baby, okay? You know that already! I just don't understand why I have to constantly remind you of my feelings. It's too much at one time to deal with, and honestly you're starting to push me away." I tried to sound stern as if I was talking to one of my kids. She needed to understand the situation she was in. She was the sidekick in this play—no more, no less.

"Jazz, I'm not trying to push you away. I just need to know that you care about me. I need to hear you say it every once in a while."

"I care about you, Monica, I really do. Do you believe me?"

"Yes, I believe you," she said between sniffles as she tried to get herself together.

"Okay, now dry those tears and straighten up that pretty face. I'll make it up to you later on tonight." I figured if I knocked her off real quick, she would chill for a bit.

"Will you stay the entire night?"

"Monica . . ."

"Okay, okay. I'm sorry, I know you can't stay. Can you at least stay until eight?"

"Sure, I'll leave work at six and come chill with you until eight, okay?"

"Eight-thirty," she pleaded from the other end.

"I'm about to change my mind," I warned her over the phone line.

"Okay, eight it is. I love you."

Instead of replying, I just hung up. This girl was going to

drive me into a white jacket by the time all of this was finished. I gathered up my documents for court and threw on
my leather jacket so I could head out. Just as I was reaching
my hand out to turn the knob the phone rang again. I
started not to answer it because I thought it was Monica
again, but I went on and took the call anyway. My secretary
was on lunch, so I had no way of intercepting the call.

"Jasmine Cinque's office," I said into the phone, praying it
wasn't some bullshit on the other end.

"Hey baby, how's your day going?" my husband inquired. I
wanted to tell him I had a lovesick stalker calling me every
five minutes to make sure I didn't stop caring about her, and
the reason why she was acting that way was because I was face
to face with her clit damn near every night. Then I'd come
home and tongue kiss him after giving my children a kiss on
the cheek. Instead, I opted for the logical answer.

"It's going okay. Right now I'm on my way out the door to
the Campbell trial. What's good?"

"Me and you, dinner at the Hibachi at six tonight."

"Tonight? Can we do it tomorrow?" I panicked a little because I just told Monica I would chill with her, and I knew if
I didn't go I would be on the phone another three hours tomorrow trying to explain to her that my husband came first
no matter how much sex we had.

"Baby, I already made the reservations," James responded
sounding kind of down.

"Okay, baby. I'll meet you there." That gave me enough
time to talk to Monica after I got out of court because I knew
I would need at least an hour to calm her down.

"Well, actually you're scheduled to take the rest of the day
off. Your boss cleared your schedule for the rest of the afternoon after your trial. I have a couple's spa set up for us, so I
will be at the courthouse waiting for you. See you there. I
love you."

He hung up before I could say anything. I didn't have time to call Monica because I would be late for my trial for sure messing around with her. I ran out to my jeep, and once I got into the flow of traffic I tried to call her. Her answering machine kept picking up, and I didn't want to be inconsiderate and just leave a message. I tried calling all the way until I got into the courthouse, and once I walked into the courtroom to represent my client I had to turn my cell phone off.

I tried to get my client out on the strength that I would shorten his probation, but the judge denied him bail because he had gotten into several fights since he'd been incarcerated and had been sent to the hole numerous times. I didn't even feel like the fight and called it a day as the judge gave him a year on top of the six he already had with a chance of making bail after three years and good behavior. That was unlikely to happen, so I promised my client I would be upstate to see him, and I left out to meet James.

I was not prepared to see what I saw when I walked out of the courthouse. Upon leaving the building and trying to find my cell phone, I looked up to see Monica and James talking by his car. I knew why James was there, but why did Monica show up? I approached them cautiously because I didn't know who would cut the hell up first.

"Baby, you remember Monica, don't you?" he asked me after he embraced me in a bear hug. Monica was shooting me dirty looks over his shoulder, and I pleaded with my eyes for her to keep cool.

"Yeah, how have you been?" I asked reaching out to shake her outstretched hand.

"I've been good. Thanks for asking," she offered, leaving my hand dangling in mid air. I pulled my hand back, a little hurt by her actions.

"Baby, she was just telling me about a young lady she's been dealing with that has her head over heels. I ran into her out here on my way to get you. She was on her way to buy her flowers for their date tonight."

"Really," I replied with a dry throat. I didn't know what type of shit Monica was trying to pull, but today I swear she would get her ass whipped.

"Yeah, she's a lawyer, too. You might know her," she replied trying to sound innocent. I wanted to black her eye on the spot.

"I might," I replied trying to change the subject. "James, don't we have reservations?"

"Yeah, we do. Monica, it was nice running into you. Be safe and I hope to see you soon."

"Yeah, both of you do the same," she replied after shaking James hand again. Maybe it was just me, but that sounded a little like a threat. I wanted to call her on it, but I didn't want to draw attention to our situation.

James walked around the car to open the door for me, and I moved to put my belongings in the back before I got in. When I looked up at her, I could see a single tear drop down her cheek before she turned and walked away. I felt like shit, but what could I do? Again, she was the sidekick in this play—no more, no less.

I was distracted during dinner and couldn't really enjoy the massage treatment at the spa because thoughts of Monica were weighing heavily on my brain. Every time James asked me what was on my mind, I told him I was thinking about the Campbell case so he wouldn't have too many questions.

Monica was just wearing me down. It's not like I was in a relationship with her, and I tried to reason with myself for treating her the way I did. Who thought a couple hundred orgasms would turn into stalker-mania? I should have known she had a screw loose when she cried that first night, but my dumb ass kept going back.

The girl was like a drug, though. She had a warm bath

ready most evenings when I got there. Whether I got in or not depended on how she acted when I walked in. Yes, I said walked in, because she gave me a key to her place. I know I shouldn't have taken it, but she started crying then, too. She would often have a meal cooked, or would feed me grapes or strawberries. She treated me like a queen, something James didn't do.

Now, don't get it twisted. James was doing well in the dick-Jasmine-down department. He was keeping up his stamina, and it seemed as though the days of the five-minute brother never existed. He was good to me. We went out often, and he surprised me with little gifts here and there. James gave me all the material possessions I could hold and more.

Monica, on the other hand, spoiled me. She catered to my every sexual need without me having to instruct her on what I wanted done. She always had a different way of pleasing me that amazed me every time. She gave me backrubs after my many long work hours, and made sure I was fresh and clean before I left her home. All of that came with a price, of course. Some days she would cry and holler at the top of her lungs because she wanted me to stay. I guess going with her to Vegas for the weekend that one time made her think I could stay like that on a regular basis.

A few times she got on the floor and wrapped herself around my legs so I wouldn't go. I had to practically drag her across the floor before she let go, and when she did she would lay right where I left her and cry. The next day I would go over and kiss her rug burns left from me having to drag her across the carpet the day before, and we would be right back to square one.

Emotionally, she was way too much for me to handle. I wanted out, but I also wanted to stay in. It's hard to explain, and every time I thought she would act right, she would start to cut up again.

I think her seeing me with James that day might have made her snap. She was truly in love with me, and it was a shame because I wouldn't allow myself to love her back. It wasn't fair to my husband or our children, and I just wasn't having it. I just hoped she wouldn't start leaving dead rabbits on my doorstep or playing on my phone or whatever it is stalkers do to get back at their mates. I wasn't in the mood, and I had to find a way to end it . . . for a little while, at least.

After dinner, James and I went to the movies, and only ended up seeing half of it before I started riding him in the back of the nearly empty theater. We were into the film, or at least I was. James kept kissing me behind my ear and fondling my breasts through my shirt. At one point he reached between my legs and stroked my clit until he had to kiss me to keep me from moaning too loud. There were only about twelve of us in the theater, but we were the only ones sitting in the back.

To make up for my stank attitude at dinner, I removed his fingers from between my legs and placed them in my mouth to remove any juices from them. Then I tongue kissed him so that he could taste it because that is a major turn on for him. While doing so, I removed his erection from his pants and began to stroke him softly. I ended the kiss to wrap my lips around him, and his head met the wall as soon as my tongue met him.

I traced the head of his penis before taking him into my mouth completely. He touched the back of my throat with no effort, and I made sure to keep his testicles warm in my small hands. He held me by the back of my neck, pushing me down on him, and I silently thanked God for giving me skills because an amateur baby-drinker would have choked.

I released his hold on my head and straddled him with my back facing him. I sat all the way down on his length, only lifting up a little before he was back in me. He held me by

my waist as he met me stroke for stroke until he exploded inside me. It was the best five minutes I ever had. Afterwards,
he wiped me as best he could with the few napkins we had
from the popcorn, and instead of letting the movie finish,
we got into the car to go home. On the way home we
stopped the car and parked behind a Dunkin Donuts where
he bent me over the hood and handled his business. We continued our session in the shower and finished up in the bedroom where we got it on for like two hours. By morning I felt
like I had ran a triathlon, but it was worth it.

I got up early and made breakfast while James was taking a
shower. Me and the kids were at the table eating by the time
he came downstairs. He looked tired, but thoroughly satisfied as he kissed me on the lips before taking the seat across
form me.

"Oooooh, mommy and daddy kissin'," my four-year-old
daughter Jaden said, covering her mouth in a cute giggle.
Jalil, her fraternal twin brother, just giggled and continued
to eat his French toast sticks.

"That's because mommy and daddy love each other, ain't
that right, honey?" James asked after giving Jaden a kiss on
the cheek and Jalil a pound. We were like the Cleavers in
there that morning.

"Yep," I replied nonchalantly. I was itching to call Monica
and was trying to hurry them out of the house.

"Daddy, can you take us to school?" our son replied as he
crammed eggs into his mouth. I was just about to ask James
that very question, but it sounded a lot better coming from
Jalil.

"Sure, buddy. I'll drop you off," James said as he stood up
to gather his belongings, "Last one to the car is a rotten
egg."

Both of our kids jumped up, neglecting the rest of their
breakfast, and ran to their rooms to get their jackets and

back packs. While they were upstairs, James stooped down beside me. He just kind of looked into my eyes like he was trying to read my thoughts. I looked back, not wanting to seem like I was nervous about anything. He looked like he wanted to say something, but instead kissed me softly on my lips. I was just about to slip him some tongue when the kids came back into the kitchen.

"They kissin' again," Jaden tried to whisper to Jalil as they walked around the table to the door. James smiled at me and pecked me on my lips one final time before standing.

"Give Mommy a hug so we can go," James instructed our children as he took one last piece of bacon off the table. They both hugged me around the neck and kissed my cheeks. I kissed and hugged them back, and I could hear Jalil tell Jaden that you got cooties from kissing as they walked out of the door. James was going to have a time with them this morning.

Before leaving out for work, I decided to go ahead and call Monica up so she could say what she had to say and get it over with. I tried to prepare myself for the tears I knew would come, but her tears made me weak. I couldn't think straight and hold a level head when she was hurting. Although I came at her strong, it tore me up on the inside to see her like that. I was determined not to fall for her, and it took everything in me to hold it down. I had two kids to think about, and my career was not to be messed with. James was also the love of my life, and I married him for better or worse. Something like that could snatch everything away from me, and that wasn't happening.

I had an hour and ten minutes before I had to be at work, so I decided to call Monica and get it over with. I knew I would need at least a half hour to deal with her. I got comfortable on the loveseat before I made my call, and decided that I would just get right to the point and let her know we couldn't see each other anymore. I reasoned that she had to be tired of me canceling on her all the time, and I was tired of the entire scenario anyway. I couldn't swing two lovers, and I knew my best bet was to stay with my husband.

When I called her, she picked up on the first ring. I didn't have time to practice what I was going to say, and she caught me off guard a little. She didn't sound too upset, and that had me shook. If anything, she sounded too damn cheerful.

"Hey, Monica, it's me," I breathed into the phone. I was hoping to make a clean break, and didn't want her to start getting all hysterical on me.

"Hey, Jazz, what's good? What can I do for you?" I had to look at the phone for a minute to make sure I was talking to the right person. This didn't sound like the Monica I knew.

"Well, about yesterday . . ."

"Don't sweat it; it's cool," she just cut me off on some real nonchalant shit. I didn't know whether to be happy she was chillin' or ask her what the hell was going on.

"Okay, well, if you want I can make it up to you tonight."

"It's cool, no worries," she just kind of mumbled into the phone. Something was definitely up. I figured I might as well break the news to her so that we could be done with it. She didn't seem interested anymore anyway.

"I get off work at five tonight. Can we talk then?

"Actually, I was just about to call you to give you your dismissal papers."

"Excuse me?" *I know this chick isn't dissin' me.* I was starting to get an attitude.

"I've decided I'm done with this situation. After yesterday I realized it just wasn't worth it. So, you're dismissed." And she was serious.

"Are you kidding me?" I asked in disbelief. I knew this is what I wanted, but I didn't think it would go down like that.

"No, and actually I have to tend to my company, so I'll see

you around. Don't worry about calling me back. After today this number won't work." Then she just hung up.

I must have sat on the couch looking stupid for like ten minutes. I knew I wasn't just handed my walking papers by needy ass Monica! Then she had the nerve to get ignorant with the shit. I called back to give her a few choice words, but when her phone rang the operator informed me she had blocked my number. I tried calling from my cell phone, and that was blocked too. I had a numb feeling all over my body that I couldn't quite shake as I readied myself to leave for work. In a sense I was glad it was all over, but I was a tad bit salty because I didn't think it would end like that.

Camera Shy

$\mathcal{I}$t's been one hell of a day. My morning started off all wrong, and it's been going downhill ever since. James woke up with a pissy attitude, and has been for the last four months. It's almost like him and Monica had the same shit for breakfast, because about three weeks after me and her parted, his attitude went from sugar to shit. Every time I asked him what was up, he gave me short, one-word answers and some bull about being stressed out at the news station. I tried to be peaceful, but I didn't feel like the aggravation, so I just stayed away from him.

What pissed me off the most was I would still try to be courteous and make him breakfast when I fixed the kids and me some, but he would walk in the kitchen, kiss the kids goodbye, and leave like I didn't even exist. I asked him on a couple of occasions what the hell his problem was, and he would just act like he didn't hear me say a word to him. So I just said "fuck it," and let it be.

I started to sleep in the guest room, but since me sleeping next to him made him miserable, I made sure to lay my head

there every night and stayed with my ass on his side of the
bed for good measure. I would throw my legs over his and
elbow him in his ribs just to be smart, knowing damn well I
was nowhere near sleep and it just pissed him off. When he
would finally get out of the bed to go to the bathroom or
something, I would stretch out in the middle so he would
only have the edge to sleep on when he got back.

Instead of his stubborn ass asking me to move over, he
would ball up on the very edge so he wouldn't have to touch
me, and I would move closer to him so he had no choice.
After a while he would get so frustrated that he would either
lay on the floor beside the bed or go into the den and rest
because he claimed it was too cold in the guest room. Who
cared? If I had it my way I would pack the hell up and be
over there with Monica in a heartbeat, but this wasn't television, so it wouldn't go as smoothly as that. I didn't want to,
but every so often I would find myself thinking about Monica.

One day I wasn't even paying attention and was just driving home. Well, I thought I was driving home, but when I
looked up I was sitting in front of Monica's house. Since she
played me, I decided I wasn't going to deal with her anymore, but deep down I really did care about her. I just couldn't
leave my family out of nowhere, and I don't think she understood that.

I started to just pull off when I noticed her porch light
come on. I didn't want her to think I was a Peeping Tom or
anything like that, so I started to put my Blazer in drive. For
some reason my foot wouldn't step on the gas. I tried to be
out, but my body wouldn't let me go. Before I knew it, she
was down her steps and looking through the passenger side
window.

I rolled down the window and looked at her. *She's even pret-
tier than I remember,* I thought, and all of the good times we
had flooded my mind. We looked at each other for what felt

like an eternity before I got out of the jeep and walked
around to where she was. Without any hesitation we stepped
into each other's arms, and my tears flowed instantly. I cried
because things were a mess at home and I felt powerless in
trying to fix it. My heart hurt because I hurt her, and to my
surprise I wasn't ashamed to admit that I was in love with
her. I had been for some time, but I still couldn't say it.

"Let's go in the house and talk for a while," she offered as
we stepped back from each other.

"Sure, let's do that," I responded through watery eyes and
a weak smile. I didn't even realize I cared this much about
her until we came face to face, and I hoped we could come
to some kind of understanding before the night was over.

Her home was still beautiful, and I felt at peace when I sat
down in her living room. Just like old times, she sat at the
other end and gave me a foot massage while we talked. I didn't
want to end up with her head between my legs, so I kept my
thighs tight so that she wouldn't get any ideas. I was trying to
clear my heart of some pain, and I really needed her to listen.

"So, do you think he's cheating on you?" Monica inquired
while she worked her magic on my calves. Who knew someone with such soft hands could get a firm grip the way she
does? I felt like putty in her hands, literally.

"I never even thought about it. Out of nowhere he started
acting all crazy like the mere sight of me was killing him. A
few times he was back to his usual five minutes, but it was
only in the morning. Then when it got to be every time we
had sex I asked him what the deal was."

"And what did he say?" she asked, sounding concerned.
Meanwhile, her massage had found its way halfway up my
thighs, and her fingers were damn near dipping inside me.

"He didn't say anything. He just gave me a dirty look and
walked out of the room."

"Hmm, I don't know what to say about that. You know I would never do you that way."

"Is that so?" I asked just to be smart. I was trying not to go there, but she pushed me into it.

"Basically . . . My love for you is unconditional. I just wish I could get the same in return."

"If it's like that, why did you brush me off the way you did when you came to the courthouse that day?" That was the million-dollar question I'd wanted to know the answer to for months.

"At that point I was just tired," she responded with a sad look on her face. I waited for her to continue, but she just went on with her massage.

"Okay, do you care to elaborate?"

"Well, even though I knew you had a family already, I still hoped that it could just be you and me exclusively. I know James is wonderful in the bedroom, but I pay more attention to your needs than he does. You never have to worry when it comes to me and satisfaction." She had a point there.

"Monica, I know all that, and that's why I love you. I just need you to understand that. What's wrong?"

Tears were threatening to fall from Monica's pretty eyes, and I had no idea as to why.

"You said you love me. Do you know how long I've been waiting for you to say that? I didn't think it would ever happen."

"Monica, I love you. I just need you to understand that I have a husband and kids at home. I just can't up and roll out like that. It's not just my life at stake here."

"Jazz, I know that. All I'm asking is that we get to see each other more often. James wouldn't know. He would think we're just hanging out. I just need you to be around."

"Monica, I wish it was that easy."

I didn't want to love her, but I did. Now I was all confused and I didn't know what move to make next. Who thought that me, Jasmine Cinque, would ever love someone of the same sex?

"It can be if you would just try it. The least you can do is think about it. That's all I'm asking you to do."

"Look, I'll think about it, but you have to promise to give me time to do just that. Give me room to make decisions, and don't crowd me like you usually do. All that does is push me away."

"I can do that. Just keep loving me."

"I will."

She kissed me softly on the lips while her hands explored the rest of my body. I was dripping wet by the time her fingers made contact with my clit, and I wanted more. Usually she did me first, but tonight I felt like getting into trouble. I pulled her thong to the side, and motioned for her to lie back on the couch. She put one leg over the back of the couch, and the other on the floor as I made myself comfortable between her legs.

I inserted two fingers into her and sucked on her clit softly the way she liked it. She grinded her opening into my face, and her body shook as she released herself on my tongue. That was amazing because I hadn't been down there that long. She was moaning like crazy, and just to make it up to her for being nasty toward her, I pushed her legs up so that they were touching her chest and dipped my tongue into her asshole until she exploded again. She had to practically beg me to stop, and I did after she had her fifth orgasm.

Monica got up off the couch on wobbly legs and asked me to follow her upstairs. I thought we were going into the bedroom, but she walked passed that door and went into the one at the end of the hallway. When she opened the door and flicked the switch, the room seemed to glow from my viewpoint. Upon entrance I saw that she had several cameras set up ready to take pictures. The room was all white, with a few photos here and there.

"Take off your clothes, and lay right there," she said pointing to a large area rug in the center of the room.

"Monica, I am not in the mood for taking pictures," I said, a little irritated. Shit, I was ready for back-to-back orgasms. We could play "photographer" another day.

"Just a couple, I promise. These are for my private collection so I can look at you when you're not here."

"Let me end up on the Internet, and see what happens," I said to her as I disrobed and made myself comfortable on the floor.

"Panties too," she said, pointing at my thong.

"I thought I could get away with that," I smiled sheepishly as I took them off and tossed them where my clothes were laying.

"Now, I want you to relax. Look seductive, as if I'm tasting you right now. Play with yourself and cum for the camera. The flash is off so it won't distract you. Just act like I'm not even here."

I started out leaning up on my elbow and stroking my clit. I held my lips open with my thumb and middle finger while my forefinger dipped into my cave and teased my clit. My eyes were closed. My head rolled back. Thoughts of James kept trying to surface, but I blocked them out and pretended my finger was Monica's tongue.

In the background I could hear Monica make comments on how I was doing, and she got so close a few times I thought she took a picture of my uterus or something. I could feel the camera lens press against me. I spotted a bowl of wax fruit and vegetables on a table in the corner, and walked over to see what I could use. Selecting and oversized cucumber, I stretched back out and continued my journey.

Using the cucumber made for some very interesting pictures.

"Let's take this to the shower."

I got up without saying a word and followed her to her bedroom. She was still snapping pictures as I bent over to turn the shower on and then fixed my hair in a bun so it wouldn't get wet. After adjusting the water temperature, I stepped under the steady stream and began to seductively lather my body with the loofah that was resting on the side. I sucked on my own nipples, moaning in the process. She was moaning too, but she never put the camera down.

After a few more shots she joined me and we devoured each other until the water got cold. Monica dried me off and laid me on the bed, and I fell asleep instantly when my head touched the pillow. I only planned to sleep for a little while, then I would go home. I knew taking the photos was a bad idea, but I wanted to make her happy. I didn't think she would use them against me, but that just goes to show how much you really don't know a person. I woke up to her kissing me on my stomach an hour later. Stretching to get the kinks out, I smiled down at her as she made her way down toward my feet.

"Sleep well?" she asked, helping me sit up on the side of her bed.

"Yes I did. Thanks for asking."

I got up and noticed that my clothes were folded neatly in the lounge chair by the door. I walked over and started to get dressed. Once again I couldn't find my panties, and had to wonder what was up. *Was this an invasion of the panty snatchers or something?* It was like I was losing a sock in the dryer or something.

"Monica, have you seen my panties? They're not over here."

"Yes, I put them away for safe keeping."

"I need to put them on. I can't go home without panties on. James will know I was out doing something I had no business doing."

"I need them. That's all I have of you when you're away."

"That's fine, but every time I come here you keep them. You must have at least ten pairs of my underwear. How many memories do you need?" I was still getting dressed while we were talking, minus the undergarments. I just knew I needed to get home, and I didn't have time to argue.

"Are you mad at me?" she asked like she was about to cry.

"No, sweetie. I'm not mad, I just want you to keep what we talked about in mind."

"I am. I just wish you could stay."

I gathered my suit jacket and hair barrette and made my way downstairs. She followed behind me slowly and I waited impatiently by the door although my face didn't show it. I wanted to scream for her to move a little faster, but I didn't want to hurt her feelings. When she got to the door she had tears on her cheeks, and I wanted to drop my bag and never leave, but I had to go.

"Monica, don't do this to me. I need you to be understanding."

"I'm fine, I just miss you already."

"I'll be back, and I'll call you when I get home. Just don't cry, okay?"

"You do love me, right?"

"Yes, Monica, I love you."

"Okay, drive safely."

"I will, and I'll call you."

She watched me until I got to my car. I waved at her as I pulled off and jetted home to be with my family.

I said I didn't want this, but for some reason I couldn't walk away. She wouldn't let me. An old saying that my grandmother used to say to me came to mind as I went well past the speed limit on the expressway: *The first time you hurt me, it's shame on you. The second time, it's shame on me. All the times after that is plain foolishness.* I felt like a fool too. I knew that all this would blow up in my face sooner or later. What you do in the dark will come out in the light whether you want it to or not.

When I got home, James and the kids were in the den watching *Finding Nemo* on DVD. I kissed the kids on the cheek and said hello to James. He gave me a weak response, never taking his eyes off the television. I wasn't in the mood for his bullshit, so I went on upstairs and hopped in the shower. When I came out, he was already in the bed reading a magazine. I tried my best to ignore him as I moisturized my body so I could put some nightclothes on and chill. I saw him peeking at my naked body, and I also saw him rise to the occasion. *He better go to the bathroom and get to whacking, because ain't shit poppin'.*

I stepped into my knee-length chemise and climbed under the covers. Turning my back to him, I chilled on my side and closed my eyes, thinking about how I was going to deal with Monica. I almost didn't hear him talking to me until he repeated his question for the third time.

"What did you say?" I asked with my back still facing him. I wanted this to be quick and done with.

"I asked how was work?"

"Fine," and left it at that. He still wanted to talk, and I felt like we were playing *Jeopardy* with all the questions he was throwing at me.

"Is the case coming along okay?"

"Yeah."

"What's with the short answers?" he said, a tad agitated. I didn't even give a damn, and told him just that.

"I've been wondering that same thing for the past four months."

"I told you I was stressed at work."

"That's the same excuse I have then."

"You weren't at work. I called there six times."

"And, what? You're checking up on me now?"

"No, it's not like that."

"Then what is it like? You've been giving me your ass to kiss for months. Now all of a sudden you care about my well-being? James, please tell that shit to someone who gives a damn."

"I do care, I've just been going through stuff."

"I tried to help you."

"I know that, and I apologize. I just don't want to lose you to someone else."

"Like who, James?" I started to sweat a little because I thought maybe he found out about me and Monica, but I wasn't going to be the one to say it first.

"I don't know who, but I need to know that it's just me and you."

I turned to face him and asked with a straight face, "Have I ever cheated on you before?"

"No, but . . ."

"Then I have no reason to now."

"Are you sure?"

"Are you? Usually when you start pointing the finger it's you who's doing it."

"I would never do that."

"Neither would I."

"Then how come we haven't been having sex lately?"

"Because you've been acting shitty. That five minutes you dishing out I can do myself," I regretted it as soon as it left my lips.

"So, is that how it is? Is that what you think of me?"

"James, it's not like that."

"If it wasn't like that, you wouldn't have said it," he responded while he put on the sweat suit he had on earlier.

"James, why are you leaving?"

"I just need to clear my head. I'll be back. The kids are still watching the movie, check on them in another half hour."

I was left speechless with a dumb-ass look on my face as he walked out of the bedroom. I heard him get in the car and pull away, and I resisted the urge to jump in my Blazer and go after him. I wanted to, but I couldn't leave the kids by themselves, and by the time I would've gotten dressed and got them to the neighbor's, he would be long gone. Besides all that, I didn't want the neighbors in my business. I just sat on the bed and thought about the last couple of months and what our future held. At this rate it didn't look too bright, and I was hoping our vows, *for better or worse,* held up.

How It All
Went Down . . .

Playing With Fire

James pulled up in front of Monica's house after riding around in circles for two hours. Just like Jasmine, he had no intentions of ever seeing Monica again. The creeping they had been doing for the past four months had started to wear him down and his relationship with Jasmine was suffering. Taking all of that into consideration, he walked slowly up the path to Monica's house. Standing outside the door hesitant to ring the bell, he finally leaned on it until she answered. He had no business being there, this he knew. He felt terrible, but the things his wife said made him feel even worse. He knew that if no one else in the world could make him feel wanted, Monica would.

When she opened the door, a pleasant smile spread across her face. She didn't expect to see James this evening, especially since she just had his wife earlier. Standing in front of him in crotchless, French cut boy-shorts and three-inch stiletto heels, she waited for him to stop staring at her exposed breasts and make contact with her eyes before she said anything.

"What do I owe the pleasure of seeing your handsome face this evening?" she purred in his ear as she ran her hands up under his shirt and across his nipples. James tried to act like he wasn't fazed by her actions, but his evident erection spoke volumes.

"I needed to get out of the house. Jazz is trippin' again," he said, remembering his reason for being out that time of night. His erection faded to nothing as he stood with his head bowed down, waiting for Monica to invite him in.

"Really?" she responded as if she hadn't seen Jasmine since the courthouse incident. "Want to come in and talk about it?"

"Yeah," he said stepping into her living room, brushing against her to get by.

Monica already had her mind set on getting some before he left and made sure that he knew it too. Before he knocked on the door, Monica was upstairs entertaining Sheila, Jasmine's secretary from the law firm. Neither Jasmine nor Sheila knew about each other, and that made for a perfect playing field for Monica. With Jasmine she got her cake, James gave her the ice cream, and Sheila was the cherry on top. It would make for the perfect sundae if she could get them all together at one time.

They sat down in the living room and she removed his sneakers before placing his feet in her lap and giving him a foot massage. He went into detail about what happened with Jasmine and how their sex life was next to nothing since he had been dealing with Monica. He went into how he didn't think he could continue the affair with Monica because he needed to make his home life work.

"Honestly, I don't know what to do," he said to Monica in a defeated voice.

"You know what your problem is?" she asked him softly.

She didn't want to ruffle any feathers because she wanted to at least sex him one more time before he decided to stay away. She honestly didn't think they would hook up again after the threesome she talked him into having with Jasmine, but it kind of just worked out that way. He dropped three thousand on that night, and the money just kept coming. When he gave her the money for the threesome, that was supposed to be it, but months later he still found himself paying for her services.

"My problem?" he responded, sounding annoyed. "Why do I have to have a problem?"

"James, relax. I'm not saying a problem like that. I'm just going to point out what you're doing wrong. Shall I continue?"

"Please do!" he looked like he was ready to leave. After all, he hadn't come there to hear what he was doing wrong; he knew what he was doing was unacceptable.

"The issue is your sex life has changed at home, right?"

"Yeah, she doesn't do what you do. Not to say that she's not good, but with you it's always something new."

"Does she have sex with you every time you want it?"

"Yeah, even when she doesn't," James said, wondering where this conversation was going.

"Are you still doing the same things for her that you used to? And don't lie," Monica warned him. Her massage was now up to his calves, and James was having a hard time concentrating.

"I like to think so."

"The thing is, James, when a man cheats on wifey, he tends to neglect her because he's concentrating on his new toy. What you don't realize is your wife can do the same things I do, probably better if you took your time with her. Don't change up your sexual habits with her because all you can think about is how good I'll fuck you. That's exactly how wives always find out that men are cheating. You change, and that's not good."

"So what am I supposed to do?" he asked, wanting desperately to make things right.

Monica was good to him. James couldn't deny that, but Jasmine was his wife, the mother of his kids, his soul mate. He couldn't see messing up everything they'd built together over a booty call.

"After you're done here, go home and make up with your wife. Don't rush it, but let her see that you're changing. You can have your cake and eat it too. You just have to know when to do it."

"I understand that, but are you going to be okay with us not seeing each other for a while? I don't want to hurt you."

"I'm cool with it. I have someone else occupying my time right now. Want to go upstairs and unwind before you go home?"

"Do you think I should?"

"I don't see why not. You won't be here for a while, so you might as well get one for the road."

Monica stood up and walked towards the stairs. James followed like a little puppy dog, feeling kind of guilty on the inside. He started seeing Monica months before he brought Jasmine in on the threesome. He told himself that after they got together in the hotel that night he would be leaving Monica alone, and he did try. Monica just had a way of making you feel like you were missing out on something when she wasn't around.

He looked at the drawings on the wall as they walked by, and stopped when he noticed one of the men in the drawings looked like him. In the drawing he was laying on his back on pink roses, and Monica was riding him with her back facing him. Her head was thrown back and her arm rested on his chest for support. Monica's hair was long in the drawing and a rose rested at her temple. James didn't know what to say; he just kind of stood there gazing at it.

Monica made her way to the top of the steps and yelled for James to hurry up. He tore his gaze from the drawing and made his way up the stairs, a little puzzled at how he became a part of her collection. He knew Monica was an artist and that she drew black art and sold it for high dollars. He also knew she was a professional photographer and took pictures for a number of agencies. He never thought he would be in one of them, and was going to question her once they got in the bedroom.

When he walked into the bedroom, all thoughts of him questioning Monica left his mind as he laid eyes on Sheila. He remembered her face, but couldn't think of where he'd seen it. He was also stunned because he didn't know Monica had company. He wished he would come home one day and find Jasmine in his bedroom with a beautiful woman. He also knew Jasmine didn't get down like that, and that she only dealt with Monica that night to make him happy. James didn't have the nerve to ask her to do it again.

"Hello, so glad you could join us," Sheila said before she kneeled down on the side of the bed between Monica's legs. Monica closed her eyes and leaned her head back, enjoying the tongue-lashing Sheila was giving her. James undressed immediately then walked over and joined them on the bed.

He kissed Monica's lips briefly before finding his way to her chocolate nipples. Sheila's mouth had already wrapped around his erection, and he almost exploded instantly when her tongue ring made contact with the head of his dick. He remembered thinking she was better than Monica before he laid back on the bed, allowing Monica to sit on his face.

Monica held her lips apart as James flicked and sucked her clit until she came in his mouth. Standing up on the bed

she motioned for him to move back so that his entire body
was on the bed comfortably. Switching places, Monica straddled his length and Sheila sat on his face. The two women
kissed and fondled each other until they all exploded together. James's seed dripped out of Monica when she stood
up off him.

In the shower he was beating himself up on the inside because he never ever had sex with her without protection. He
never bothered to ask Monica if she was on any type of birth
control and feared it was too late to inquire now because he
knew she would be offended. Sheila and Monica scrubbed
him clean and helped him dress so he could get home.

"Where are my boxers?" he asked Monica while Sheila was
putting his socks on his feet.

"I put them away for safe keeping," she responded nonchalantly as she pulled his undershirt over his head. Sheila
already had his pants halfway up and was waiting for him to
stand so that she could finish the job.

"Every time I come here you keep my boxers. What do
you have now? About ten or twelve pair?" he asked, a little
annoyed. He could not go home without any underclothes
on, and hoped his credit card was in the car so he could stop
and get some on the way back.

"That's all I have to keep you close to me," Monica responded as she pushed him toward the front door.

When they got downstairs, he turned to get one last look
at her. He gazed into her eyes and then down at the rest of
her body, stopping at the red lace boy-shorts she had on.
Kissing her one last time, he looked down at her underwear
again, trying to remember if he'd seen them before.

"You know, my wife has a pair of panties just like these," he
said while pulling lightly at the band around her waist.

"She has good taste," Monica said, smiling up at him.

"Yeah." James looked at the door and then turned to face

Monica again. "About that drawing on the wall . . . I don't re-member posing for it."

"You didn't. I remembered one of the nights you were here, and decided to put it on canvas. Is that okay?" she asked, daring him to say otherwise. If he had said it wasn't cool, she would have sent it to Jasmine in the mail to let her know he had been there. Lucky for him, he didn't have a problem with it.

"No, it's cool. Just don't let it get out, okay? You know, with my career and all," he said, his voice slightly quivering.

"It won't, now go home," Monica said while opening the door. She wanted James out, and he was starting to get on her nerves. James had already served his purpose. She didn't need him anymore, so there was no use in wasting her time talking to him about shit she didn't care about.

"One more question then I'm gone."

"What, James?" Monica spat at him, her annoyance show-ing.

"Is that woman Jasmine's secretary?"

"Yes, why do you ask?" she replied with a slight smile on her face.

"She won't tell will she? I don't want any trouble with them on the job."

"No, your secret is safe. Now go home!"

"Okay, okay. I'm going. I miss you already."

"Yeah, yeah. I miss you too, now go."

James slowly made his way to the car, trying to make sense of what had just happened. With him exploding inside of Monica and orally pleasing his wife's secretary, he was sure this wasn't the end of it. He just prayed he could fix things at home before shit got out of hand.

Sheila listened to everything from the top of the stairs and crept back to the room when she heard Monica closing the front door. She liked Jasmine as a person and didn't want anything to do with this bullshit Monica had cooking up. This was only her second time at Monica's house, and she was still surprised at how she ended up there the first time. She was sitting on the edge of the bed contemplating all of this when Monica walked in the room.

"So, Sheila, did you enjoy yourself tonight, sweetie?" Monica asked before she reached behind the mirror and pulled out the camcorder. Sheila didn't know they were being taped and didn't know what to do. She'd just gotten herself into some serious shit and was clueless as how to get out of it.

"Yes, it was nice, but I need to be heading out. I need to pick up my son from my mom's house before she starts calling around looking for me." Her son was at home with her sister, but she was trying to find any reason to leave. She knew she would never step foot into Monica's house again, but she had to get out first.

"No problem, sweetie. Call a cab and get yourself dressed. I want to download some of these pictures onto my laptop before I forget. Let me know when you're leaving," Monica replied before leaving the room. She never even made eye contact with Sheila as she talked.

Sheila got dressed as quickly as possible after calling a cab from Monica's phone. She sat in the living room as she was instructed, and didn't budge until the cab driver honked his horn out front. Monica came into the living room and gave her money to get home in one envelope and money for the evening in another. Sheila was confused as to why she was getting paid for being there, and it showed all over her face.

"Now, this night is our little secret, right?" Monica warned more than asked Sheila as she waited for her to reply.

"Yes, I won't say anything."

"Okay, I'll call you later. Be sure to answer the phone."

Sheila walked out of the house and Monica watched her

from the doorway, not seeming to care that she was still topless. Just as Sheila was opening the cab door, Monica called
out to her. Sheila looked at Monica puzzled at what she was
calling her for.

"Just a heads up," Monica began with an evil look on her
face. "Don't fuck with me!"

Sheila got into the cab quickly and instructed the driver to
take her home. Her heart didn't slow down for a couple of
blocks, and for once in her life someone other than her
mother put fear in her. She never suspected Monica was
crazy, just a little obsessive with all the pink and white going
on. Now that she knew Monica was crazy, she had to find a
way to tell Jasmine without her finding out she'd slept with
her husband too. Sheila didn't know what to do and was in
tears by the time she got home.

James had left his credit card in another pants pocket and
didn't have any cash on him to replace the underclothes
Monica took from him. He decided once he got in the house
that he would hop in the shower and sleep in the guest room.
He wanted to make up with Jasmine for the way he had been
acting, but tonight wouldn't work. He smelled like he just
came from Monica's house, and he didn't want Jasmine to
even think he was stepping out on her.

When he walked in Jasmine was lying on the couch asleep.
She must have been waiting for him to get back and dozed
off. Looking at his watch, he saw that he'd been gone for at
least three hours and knew that Jasmine was going to have a
fit when she woke up. He also knew that if he tried to sneak
past her and hop in the shower she would definitely know
what he had done.

Stuck between a rock and a hard place, he decided to
wake Jasmine up and try to apologize to her. He stood over
her watching her sleep and silently wondered what he had

gotten himself into dealing with Monica. He knew he had to stay away or Jasmine would find out he was creeping. He honestly couldn't think of a reason to cheat on his wife, and he did feel bad. He decided at that moment that he wouldn't contact Monica anymore. From what he could see she was nothing but trouble—trouble that was easy to get into.

"Jasmine, wake up," he whispered in her ear, shaking her a little to get her attention. When she opened her eyes, she looked at him like she wanted to punch him out.

"What time is it?" she asked while she sat up on the couch and got herself together.

"It's one-thirty in the morning," James responded while bracing himself to be cursed out. Jasmine had a sharp tongue, and she could slice you up with just words.

"So you've been gone for at least three hours. Why did you leave like that without letting me explain myself?"

"Jazz, I really don't know. You hurt me."

"I hurt you? You've been acting like you hate me for the last few months. How did I hurt you?"

"I know I've been treating you wrong. I've been stressed at work and tired when I get home."

"I'm tired when I get home too, but I make sure you and the kids eat, and if you want to have sex you get it no matter how late I'm at the office. I bend over backwards to keep this house running smoothly no matter how stressed I am."

"Baby, I know, and I'm sorry about the way I've been treating you. I'm sorry I stormed out of here the way I did; I just needed to breathe for a second."

"James, I need to breathe, too. You say shit to me that I don't like but I stay here and deal with it! I just can't up and leave because I have kids to think about. Mommy can't afford to have a breakdown when things don't go right," Jasmine said between her tears, partly because she couldn't get Monica out of her system and partly because she didn't want James to go.

"I know that, Jazz. I know I need to change, but I need you to stick it out and help me. I need you to love me like you used to."

"James that will never change, but you need to get it together. I can't do this by myself."

"Baby, I know. I love you so much, and I need you. Whatever you do, just don't leave." James was begging her, nearly in tears. He had to leave Monica alone, and he vowed to himself right then that he would never be alone with her after that day.

Jasmine was a little shaken up because she had just told Monica they could chill again. She knew if she wanted to work things out with James, she had to let Monica go, but she wasn't sure she wanted to. Monica seemed to complete her, and it just sort of worked out. Jasmine knew if she called Monica and told her they couldn't get together anymore, Monica would spazz out. She was temperamental like that, and she could be dangerous if rubbed the wrong way. So Jasmine decided to just fall back instead of talking to Monica, and only see her when she could.

On the other side of town, Monica placed the photos she'd downloaded from her camcorder into a hidden safe behind the picture she drew of her and the governor of D.C. She had her hooks in his wife also, and she decided it was about time to call for her money. He paid Monica to keep quiet about him sleeping with her on occasions, and he didn't know Monica was having sex with his wife and his oldest daughter. She also knew she had to keep Sheila in check before her paranoid ass messed up everything. She had work to do, and she went to relax in the tub before putting her plan into action.

Marital Bliss?

For James, staying away from Monica was nothing. He knew she was trouble, and to avoid losing his wife he avoided her. She called his cell phone on occasion to hook up, but he always had a reason why it wasn't a good idea. This, of course, frustrated Monica, and she wasn't one to let things go easily. Deciding to pay James a little visit at home, she got into her hot pink convertible Benz dressed in a trench coat and stiletto heels. Freshly done hair, perfect make-up, and nothing underneath the trench coat was sure to get James's attention. She almost burst with anticipation as she zigzagged in and out of traffic on her twenty-minute ride to the Cinque household.

Deciding to park a block down from the house so James wouldn't hear her pull up in the driveway, Monica made her way to the front door, her heels echoing loudly on the sidewalk. Glancing through the window, she spied James sitting on the couch in boxers and a t-shirt watching television. Monica knew Jasmine and the kids were away because Sheila had informed her that Jasmine went to visit her mother in

Virginia on a three-day-weekend vacation. James couldn't go because it was sweeps week at the station, and he had to be there to make sure everything ran smoothly.

Ringing the doorbell, she loosened the belt on her coat so that when he opened the door she could surprise him. She felt in her pocket for the pair of panties she had in there then posed for him once the door opened.

"Monica, what are you doing here?" James asked as he leaned out the door and looked from side to side to make sure none of his neighbors were out. Things with he and Jasmine were starting to get better, and the last thing he needed was one of his nosey-ass neighbors seeing another woman entering his house. They would tell Jasmine no soon as she set foot on the block, and that would be something else he would have to explain. They were finally talking out their differences, and although it wasn't back to normal, it was damn close.

"I came to see you. I miss you," Monica responded, revealing herself to James. The look on his face said it all, yet he hadn't invited her in yet. Rubbing her hands down her body, she looked James in the eye, waiting for him to say something.

"I told you we had to chill for a while. I thought you understood that," James responded with his eyes still roaming all over Monica's naked body. Her trench coat was falling off her shoulders while she fingered herself. James knew if he didn't invite her in she would be standing in front of him naked for the entire neighborhood to see. And with his luck, all his neighbors would come out as soon as her coat hit the ground.

"Yeah, but Jazz and the kids are out of town, and you know what they say," she responded as she walked up to him in the doorway, and took hold of his erection. *When the cat's away . . ."*

"Monica, we can't do this. Jasmine would have a fit!" James tried to keep his cool as she was backing him into the house, but it wasn't working. Before he knew it, Monica had the door closed and him sprawled out on the couch with his boxers down around his knees.

"What she doesn't know won't hurt you. You know you want this."

She kissed him behind his ear and stroked his length against her clit at the same time. Her wetness covered the head of his penis, and James struggled to gain control of the situation.

"Monica, you shouldn't be here," James responded weakly as he pushed her back off him. He stood up, pulling his boxers up with him, and tried to clear his head. Monica was set on getting it whether he wanted to give it or not, and instead of arguing with him, she turned and went upstairs.

James was left standing in his living room with a hard dick and no idea of what to do. He went over and locked the door, hoping to God no one saw Monica come in. He knew Monica wasn't leaving until she got what she came for. He had no choice but to knock her off real quick, and decided he would get it done quickly so that she could leave.

By the time James came up to the room, Monica was spread out on the lounge chair by the window with both sets of her lips spread open. Her eyes were closed, and she didn't open them until he was right up on her.

"Monica, we have to make this quick. I don't know what time Jazz will be back, and she can't see you here!" He got down on his knees on the side of the chair so that they could talk face to face.

Instead of responding, she took her finger out of her walls and placed it in his mouth. His eyes closed as he tasted her wetness with a hint of chocolate body butter mixed in. He stood at attention immediately, and Monica moved up so the head of his penis was just inside her cave.

James moaned as her muscles contracted around his head and she grinded him slowly, not letting any more than that go in. She wrapped her legs around his waist, still not letting him fully penetrate her as she tongue-kissed his nipples and rubbed his back.

Slowly at first, they pushed and pulled on each other. Monica fed James her nipples one at a time as his strokes quickened inside of her, making her lean against the window sill for support. They moaned like crazy, and James had just begun to explode when he looked out the window and saw Jasmine's Blazer pull into the driveway.

"Monica, you have to go! Jazz just pulled up . . ."

James grabbed the Glade air freshener and started spraying the room to get the smell of sex out after pulling on his boxers. Monica grabbed one of Jasmine's blouses out of the closet and wiped the semen off her stomach leaving what was on her pubic area there. She knew if she got pregnant Jasmine would leave him.

She made her way to the kitchen, and could hear Jasmine getting the kids out of the car. James had hopped in the shower, and planned to stay there until Jasmine came upstairs looking for him like he was in there the entire time. Monica slipped out the back door just as Jasmine was opening the front, and she crept around the side of the house and down the street into her car unnoticed.

Pulling up in front of the house, Monica parked her car, grabbed the binoculars that rested on the passenger seat, and stared up at the window that led into Jasmine and James's bedroom. She watched James walk into the bedroom with a towel wrapped around his waist. Monica felt sick as she watched him embrace Jasmine and kiss her slowly. She wanted Jasmine to come home to her and to kiss her that way. Briefly, she pictured herself in Jasmine's arms, and before a tear could drop, she peeled off down the street and onto the expressway thinking of how to put plan B into motion.

James held his wife like he hadn't seen her in ages. Jasmine thought it was because they were apart for the weekend, but James was just relieved that Monica had made it out in time. He sat down on the side of the bed after he was sure Monica was gone. He saw her sitting outside the house from the window and knew kissing Jasmine would piss her off, but he didn't care as long as she was gone.

"I missed you, too," Jasmine said once James pulled back from the kiss. She smiled; she wasn't expecting this, and she was pleasantly surprised.

"What are you doing back so soon? I thought you guys weren't coming back until the evening," James said as he sat down on the bed to lotion his body. He didn't want any traces of Monica on him or in the room, and sprayed cologne on his body just to make sure.

"It started raining pretty heavy down there, so I wanted to make it back before it started to flood. You know how it is down my mom's way with the dirt roads and everything," Jasmine responded, taking a seat on the lounge chair and leaning back. Her arm fell over the side, lazily making contact with the blouse Monica used to wipe her stomach off. James spotted it, but Jasmine was already leaning over to pick it up.

Holding the shirt up and feeling the stickiness on her hand, she looked at James puzzled. James continued looking down at his legs and lotioning his body like he didn't see her pick the shirt up off the floor. He wasn't going to say anything until she asked, and he hoped he could come up with a good excuse as to why there was a sticky substance on her favorite Donna Karan blouse.

"James," she said with a little attitude in her voice holding the shirt close to his bowed head, "can you explain this to me?"

Looking up guiltily, he examined the shirt she was holding with her fingertips up to his face. He didn't really know what to say, and he didn't want to lie. He also knew he couldn't tell her he'd just finished having sex with Monica on the lounge chair she was laying on and had exploded all over her stomach when she pulled up, and just to be a smart ass Monica used her shirt to wipe off. That would get him jacked up for sure.

"Before you came I was thinking about what you did to me before you left. You know your riding skills are the bomb, and I wanted something of yours near me. I was handling business, and let off on your blouse because I didn't want to get it on the bed. I was gonna have it cleaned before you noticed it."

"Then why was it under the lounge chair?" Jasmine asked suspiciously. She thought that maybe she saw Monica's car as she was riding up the street, but she wasn't sure. She didn't know too many people with a hot pink convertible, but opted to pay it no mind. She chalked it up to just missing Monica and let it be, but now she wasn't so sure.

"Because that's where I was. You know how I do, and I would have exploded all over the place if I didn't have something to cover up with. I didn't think much about it, and was going to put it in the bag for dry cleaning when I got out of the shower. You pulled up as I was getting out, and it totally slipped my mind. I can buy you another one though, two if it'll keep you from being upset with me . . . I just missed you, that's all."

With all that said, he bowed his head down like he was in

some serious trouble and waited for Jasmine to snap.
Instead, she just threw the shirt in the hamper by the door,
and moved closer to her husband. Lifting his head up by the
chin, she kissed him, softly straddling his lap in the process.

"Okay James, it's cool. The next time use something that
didn't cost so much, please. Semen isn't all that easy to get
out of silk," Jasmine replied with a smile before standing up.
"I'm going to put the kids down for a nap, be ready to make
it up to me when I get back.

"I will," James responded as she left the room.

He didn't know how he made it out of that one, but he
knew he would be staying as far away from Monica as possible. That girl was trouble with a capital 'T', and if he didn't
play his hand right, Jasmine would leave him without thinking twice about it.

Jasmine came back in the room dressed in a pink thong
and sandals that strapped to her knee of the same color.
Hitting the power button on the stereo, the slow version of
"Sumthin' Sumthin' " from the *Love Jones* soundtrack played
right on cue. Jasmine danced her way over to the bed, sensu-
ously keeping constant eye contact with her husband. Topless,
she crawled up to him on her knees, kissing his body on the
way up. James couldn't help but think that the show he was
watching was something that Monica would do, but he was glad
to see his wife broadening her views on creative lovemaking.

Squatting down onto his erection, Jasmine rode James
slowly with her hands on the headboard for support. While
they tossed and turned into different positions, James re-
called thinking about Monica only once, and saying to himself that it was going to be one hell of a night.

Monica ate ice cream and waited for the results of the
pregnancy test she'd just taken. Who knew two minutes could
be so long? She paced outside of the bathroom door trying

patiently to wait for the timer to sound, indicating her time was up. When she got home, she did a headstand for about three minutes, hoping whatever semen was on her would find its way to her insides. Never mind most of it was rubbed off on the way home. Thinking rationally was not the issue here. Having James's baby would be a scandalous thing, but Monica could care less. She lived for drama, and scandal was her favorite pastime.

Finally the buzzer sounded, causing Monica to almost drop her dessert on the floor. Walking quickly into the bathroom, she sat her pint of Ben and Jerry's on the vanity and stared down at the test on the back of the toilet. Not sure what the line meant, she picked up the box to read the directions.

"One strip means not pregnant, two strips means baby on board," she said aloud. Looking down at the test, she only saw one line.

"This is bullshit! Is the nigga shootin' blanks or what?" Monica said to her frustrated reflection in the mirror. She knew James could make babies because he had twins now. She made sure he was inside of her the first time, and the second time he pulled out, but she still got some on her. She felt pregnant, or so went her imagination.

"Maybe the test is old," Monica said. "Who knows how long they sit in the back before they are put out for sale?"

Grabbing her jacket, she decided to go to the drugstore near her house. Pulling up with a screeching halt, Monica jumped out of the car before it stopped moving completely. Going directly to the feminine products aisle, she picked up four different brands of pregnancy tests just to make sure there wouldn't be any issues. The cashier looked at her kind of crazy as she rung the items up, and Monica gave her a "don't go there" look as she paid for her stuff and ran out of the store.

On the way home she hit ninety miles an hour, and as soon as she turned the corner to her block, a police car was right on her tail with flashing lights going off. She pulled over mad as hell and not wanting to stop, and at one point thought about jetting off. When the officer got to her car, she made sure to keep her hands on the steering wheel just in case this one was trigger-happy. She didn't want to become a statistic because of speeding and a few pregnancy tests.

"Can I help you, Officer?" Monica said to the cop standing outside her car door. She hoped he would make it quick; she had things to do.

"Ma'am, are you aware of how fast you were going?"

"No, sir I'm not. I have to pee and was in a rush to get home. I only live a few houses down on this side of the street." She gave him her most pitiful look, but he didn't seem to be buying it.

"License, insurance, and registration, please," the cop said, looking into the car window.

"Sir, please. You can't give me a ticket. I just got this car. Let me make it up to you."

"Ma'am, are you soliciting me? I'm an officer of the law, and I can lock you up for prostitution."

"I'm not a prostitute, sir! I'm just trying to get out of this ticket. I only live a few houses down. No one has to know but me and you."

The officer looked at her for a second to see if she was serious. Monica started unbuttoning her shirt, exposing her chocolate breasts to the rookie cop. Monica had already slept with most of the guys on the force, and she didn't remember seeing this one before. He started thinking about how things were terrible at home, and his evident erection let Monica know she had him hooked. That was exactly how she got the mayor to sleep with her, and her little flash trick worked here too.

"Pull up to your door and go in," the officer said. "Leave the door unlocked; I'll be coming in right behind you."

Pulling off, Monica made her way down the block and parked her car in the driveway. Doing exactly as she was told, she went inside and stripped down to nothing as she waited for the cop to come in. Forgetting about the pregnancy and her earlier dilemma, she sat on the floor in front of the fireplace with her legs open, tugging on her clit. When the cop walked in, he spotted Monica and almost came on himself right then. Undressing quickly, he joined her on the rug, his head falling directly between her legs.

"Eat up, Officer," Monica spoke to him while holding on to the back of his head.

The cop kissed his way up her stomach, inserting himself unprotected as he kissed her breasts. Not even a minute later, he spit his seed inside of her, collapsing heavily on top of her. Monica held her breath and waited for him to move.

Rolling off her, he snatched her shirt from the floor beside them, and wiped himself off before stepping back into his uniform. Monica looked up at him from the floor with a smirk on her face.

"Now, be careful how you drive for now on. I wouldn't want you to tear that pretty car up," he said as he placed his state-issued hat on top of his bald head. Looking back at her one more time, he opened the door and stepped out just as his radio sounded.

"Officer Hill, what's your location?" the captain called from the precinct.

"I'm on Bellevue and Thompson on my way to City Avenue," the police officer answered back, still staring at Monica's naked body.

"There's a three-car pile-up on Route 23. Get there ASAP; it looks a bit messy."

"Roger that, I'm on my way."

"Okay, 10-4."

"10-4."

Monica just looked at him, wishing he would hurry up and close the door. After all, she was ass-naked, and there was a cool breeze outside, even for the middle of May. Officer Hill looked back at her once more before closing the door. Getting up to lock it, Monica almost laughed aloud at his silly ass.

"He had the nerve to look like he just did something," she said on the way upstairs. Totally forgetting about the pregnancy test, she filled the tub with hot water and soaked her tired body. Jasmine and how she was going to steal her from James was still on her mind as she rinsed off and went to lie across her bed. Before she knew it, she was drifting off to sleep, already making up her mind to visit Jasmine in the morning.

The next morning Monica was parked down the street from Jasmine's house waiting patiently for James and the kids to leave. She knew they rotated mornings on who took the kids out, and she hoped it would play in her favor today. Dozing off for a minute, she woke up in time to see James and his twins get in the car and pull off. Ducking down some in her seat so he wouldn't see her when they passed by, she waited about five minutes before she got out of the car and went up to the door.

Monica was dressed similarly to what she had on for James, but this time she had on the red French-cut boy shorts that Jasmine liked to see her in. Tying the belt tighter around her waist, she rung the bell and waited patiently for Jasmine to answer. When Jasmine came to the door, all she had on was a bathrobe, and half her hair was pinned up because she was curling it. Half dressed, she still looked like a goddess to Monica, and she wanted so badly to just have her to herself.

"What are you doing here?" Jasmine asked, looking both ways to see if anyone was outside. She didn't want to have to explain to James later why Monica was there.

"I came to see you, silly," Monica replied playfully. "It's been a while since we—you know, and I decided to catch you before you left. Maybe give you something to smile about while you're at work."

"Okay, Monica, that's cool and all, but what if James were here? How would I explain that?" Jasmine said, a little frustrated although she was getting wet just thinking about what Monica would do to her.

"I figured he would be gone around this time; that's why I waited. I'm sorry if I caused a problem," Monica began looking like she was about to cry. "I just miss you, and I needed to see you, so I came over."

"Look, don't cry," Jasmine said after the first tear fell. "Come on in, but we have to be quick because I have to get to work soon."

"No problem, just lay back and let me make you feel good."

Jasmine, still a little irritated, went upstairs with Monica following close behind. Going to the bathroom to unplug her curling iron, she brushed her hair back into a bun and tied a scarf around it because she knew by the time she and Monica got done she wouldn't have time to curl her hair over.

While Jasmine was in the bathroom, Monica checked behind the bed to make sure the panties were still there. She also felt in her jacket pocket for the clay she brought with her. She knew a guy that made keys, and he told her all she needed was a good print of the key she wanted duplicated and he could make her one. She hoped Jasmine's house keys would be lying around somewhere so she could get a print, and was looking around from her spot on the bed.

Jasmine entered the room naked and took a spot on the bed next to Monica. Scooting over in the middle of the bed and spreading her legs, she waited for Monica to do whatever she was going to do. She hoped James wouldn't turn around and come back to the house for anything as Monica began at her toes and worked her way up.

Monica had already taken off her panties and had them on the side of the bed. Pleasing herself in the process, she spread open Jasmine's lips with her free hand and immediately took hold of her clit, making Jasmine explode instantly. Holding her legs up, Jasmine held on to the back of Monica's head while she devoured her. Moaning like crazy and exploding all over the place, Jasmine took her nipples into her mouth one at a time, adding to the excitement that was already playing all over her body.

Monica made sure to put her tongue inside of Jasmine, lapping up all of her honey until there was nothing left. Jasmine started squirming under her, indicating that another orgasm was fast-approaching. Taking her hand from her own clit, Monica licked off her juices before inserting her fingers inside of Jasmine's tightness. Jasmine's body was barely on the bed as she rained all over Monica's hand and tongue.

Reaching over into her coat pocket, Monica pulled out the strap-on she'd brought with her and stepped into it. Getting as close to Jasmine as possible on her knees, she threw Jasmine's legs over her shoulders, plunging into her deeply and hoping that she was doing a better job than James. Jasmine held her lips open, begging Monica not to stop. Monica threw her legs over to the side, taking her that way, with Jasmine holding on to the headboard.

"Whose pussy is this?" Monica asked in a low tone, but loud enough for Jasmine to hear her.

"It's yours," Jasmine replied between breaths. Monica was doing the damn thing to her, and she was shocked because it was almost better than what James did the night before—almost.

"Tell me it's my pussy! Say it!" Monica came back, enjoying the control she had over Jasmine at this point. If Jasmine had any doubts that a woman could please her the same or better as a man, Monica wanted to make sure that she knew she could have the best of both worlds.

"Monica, it's your pussy. It's yours, baby," Jasmine responded as Monica turned her body so that she was on her knees in the doggy style position.

"It better be."

Monica started kissing Jasmine down her back, and running her tongue up and down her spine, making Jasmine go crazy. Using some of the KY-Jelly from off the nightstand, she applied some on Jasmine's asshole, never losing her rhythm with Jasmine throwing her ass back like crazy. She slowly pushed her finger into Jasmine's ass and slowed down her stroke; Jasmine's back stiffened.

"Jasmine, just relax. I won't hurt you, just enjoy it."

Every time Monica pushed in she pulled her finger out, and vice versa building up an orgasm so big Jasmine just about passed put from the explosion. Feeling satisfied that she'd handled her business, Monica pulled out of Jasmine and stepped out of her strap-on. Jasmine was lying face down on the bed trying to catch her breath as Monica dressed. Smiling to herself, she walked around the side of the bed and kissed Jasmine on the forehead.

"I'll call you later," Monica said before leaving the room, "and I'll lock the door behind me. Don't oversleep; it's nine o'clock."

Jasmine just kind of grunted her goodbye and remained sprawled out on the bed, trying to get herself together.

When Monica got downstairs, she spotted the peg block hanging by the door. Coming closer to it, she saw several keys hanging from it. There were numerous tags listing what the keys were over each peg, and the last one that read "Spare House Keys" had two of the same keys hanging from it. She started to just take a key, but that would be too easy. Testing the key in the door to make sure it was the right one, she did as she was told and pressed the key firmly into the clay; the shape and name on the key came out perfectly. Smiling to herself, she slid the clay into one of the sandwich bags on the table and left the house whistling.

On her way back home, she went by the locksmith's office and dropped the imprint off. After knocking him off quickly, he told her she could come back and get the key that afternoon. She went home, and all of a sudden felt very sleepy and decided to take her shower after a nap. She would stop by and get the key before she made her way to the studio. She was shooting Usher for the June cover of *Essence* magazine, and she could not be late.

Jasmine finally got out of the bed a half hour after Monica left. Pulling the sheets with her, the pair of underwear that Monica planted there popped out as planned. Jasmine, not wanting James to know that Monica was there and thinking that those were the panties Monica came there in, put them in the bottom of the hamper, mentally writing herself a note to get them out later before James saw them. Already late for work, she quickly dressed and headed for the office, smiling all the way there, just as Monica said she would.

Dancing With The Devil

An hour later, Jasmine walked into the office with a smile so bright she could be the star of a Colgate commercial. Unusually friendly to everyone, she practically skipped into her office, flopping down in her chair when she got there. Not that she was a mean person, but Jasmine was very professional all the time, and it was rare that she was giddy and carefree like she was now. She didn't know Monica had it in her to turn her out like that, but she was hooked. Never in her wildest imagination did she think a girl could leave her feeling sore and completely drained at the same time, but then again Monica wasn't just "any woman," and you could never be too sure of her capabilities.

"Sheila, can I see you in my office please?" Jasmine called from the intercom. She had several meetings she needed to attend, and if Sheila could download a couple of subpoenas for her by the time she got back, it would take a few hours off her day.

When Sheila walked in, her face was red and her eyes were puffy like she had been crying all morning. Trying to hide behind her hair, she sat down with her pen and notepad ready, looking into her lap and not at Jasmine like she normally did. Monica had been harassing her all week because she was avoiding her calls, and even went as far as sending her photos of her and Jasmine's husband when they were at her house. Somehow she took her face out of the pictures and put Sheila's there as if she was the one having sex with him. All she and James did was exchange oral pleasantries; there was never any penetration between the two.

She didn't know what Monica would do, but she did know she couldn't afford to lose her job. She already felt bad about what she did with her boss's husband, and Monica was only making it worse.

"Sheila, are you okay?" Jasmine asked, concern etching her face and stealing her once-jolly mood away completely.

"I'm fine." Sheila started to cry again. "Let's just get on with the meeting."

"If you were fine, you wouldn't be sitting here in tears." Jasmine decided to ignore her attitude and go around to sit in the chair opposite of Sheila with her tissue box in hand. "I'm a lawyer, I can help you."

"It's nothing, really; just some issues I have to work through, that's all," Sheila said, trying to steer the conversation away from her. She couldn't tell her boss that her crazy lover was stalking her and had sent pictures of her and her boss's husband doing the wild thing. Even though that's not how it went down, pictures say a lot, and it was tough to deny what was right in your face.

"Sheila, whatever it is, you can tell me. I'll try my best to help you, and I know others who can also. Is it your son's father? Is he abusing you?" Jasmine went on, at the same time going through her mental Rolodex thinking of who could help Sheila out with the situation she thought Sheila might be in.

Sheila just wanted to go home. As much as she wanted to tell, Jasmine could not help her out of this one. She had to do what was necessary to get Monica off her back, and although she didn't know what her solution was just yet, she knew she had to think fast before things got out of hand.

"No, I'm fine, really. I think I may end up taking a half-day if you don't really have anything for me to do. Honestly, my head is pounding and I probably won't be any good around here anyway."

"That's not a problem. All I need you to do is pull up and send out a few subpoenas for the files in the corner over there, then you can head out. Leave me a note on top of them when you're done, and your number so I can check on you later."

"Are you sure? I can stay if you need me."

"No, Sheila, go on. Every so often a woman needs to just lie down and rest for a second. You have my cell number; call if you need me."

"I will. Are we done now?" Sheila asked, wanting to get out of Jasmine's face. She felt like shit because the one person who was showing her the most concern should be whipping her ass for sucking her husband's dick. She got up to leave before any more tears fell.

"Yeah, we're done. I'll give you a call tonight, okay?"

"Cool."

Jasmine gathered a couple of folders for some cases she had to view and put the one she was about to start with on top. On her way out the door, she walked slowly by Sheila, looking to see if she was okay. Sheila was having a heated debate over the phone, and it was getting loud. Knowing how the senior partners were and not wanting Sheila to lose her job because of her personal problems, she waited by Sheila's desk for her to end the call.

"I told you to stop calling here!" Sheila said sharply

through the phone. Monica was getting on her last nerve, and she had already hung the phone up twice on her. Something Monica said made Sheila freeze up. She was holding the phone tightly to her ear, tears streaming down her face.

Jasmine touched her shoulder to let her know she was standing there, and that she was starting to get weird looks from the other workers in the office. Sheila held up one finger to indicate she was almost done with her conversation, and she wanted to talk to her.

"I'll meet you there, but this is the last time," she said to Monica on the phone.

"Be there or else," Monica said then hung up.

Sheila placed the phone back on the hook slowly and followed Jasmine back into her office. After twenty minutes of convincing Jasmine that she would be okay, Jasmine recommended that she take some time off to get herself together. She informed Sheila of the procedures for a sick and a personal leave, and told her to let her know what she would do by the next day.

"I'm just looking out for you," Jasmine said while offering Sheila more tissue for her never-ending tears.

"I know, and I really appreciate it. If you could get the paper work for me, I'll come in tomorrow and fill it out so you can put it through." Not that Sheila wanted to leave work, but Monica was too much to handle emotionally and physically, and if any shit went down between Monica and Jasmine's husband, she didn't want to be there for it.

"No problem, just go on home. I'll get one of the temps to do the subpoenas for me and we'll talk tonight, okay?"

"Okay," Sheila responded after giving Jasmine a hug.

Sheila gathered her stuff and followed Jasmine out to the elevator. On the way down to the street level, Jasmine offered her a ride to wherever she needed to go.

"That's okay," Sheila said. "You've already been a big help."

"Just let me know if you need anything."

"I will."

As the elevator doors opened, Sheila tried to quickly step through them and managed to bump her right arm against the door. She winced and dropped the folder she was carrying. The photos Monica sent her scattered across the floor.

Both women bent down at the same time to pick them up, but before Jasmine had a chance to put her hand on one Sheila scooped them all up in a big pile. Jasmine peeped a few, but not close enough to notice her husband in any of them. Jasmine handed Sheila the hat she dropped.

"You sure you don't need a ride?" Jasmine asked one last time.

Sheila pulled the folder close to her chest. "Yeah," she muttered. "I'll just take the bus." She waved, turned, and walked off.

By the time Sheila got to Monica's house, she was a nervous wreck. She opted to take the bus over there for two reasons. One because she needed time to clear her head; she had to put Monica in her place, or at least try to. She was determined to make Monica understand that she wanted no parts of the bullshit she was brewing up and that she wanted to be left out of the entire situation. The second reason she caught the bus was because she knew Jasmine and Monica were cool—not exactly how cool they were—but she knew they were friends and she didn't want Jasmine to know she was chillin' with Monica like that.

Walking up the block slowly, Sheila made her way to the only pink house on the block. Monica's house stood out, seeming to make the neighborhood look a little brighter.

Approaching the door, she raised her hand to knock. Monica swung the door open before Sheila's fist could make contact with the wood, and she accidentally punched Monica in the mouth. Monica immediately covered her mouth with both hands, caught off guard by the blow. She knew it was an accident by the look on Sheila's face, but she snapped anyway.

"Monica, I'm so sorry." Sheila reached out to hold Monica's face, but Monica stepped back. The hit wasn't as hard as Monica was making it out to be, but being the drama queen that she was, she milked it for all it was worth.

Instead of answering, she just turned around and went toward the kitchen to get some ice for the non-existent swelling she thought would take place. Sheila was so close on her heels that when Monica stopped suddenly Sheila bumped into her, causing the back of Monica's tennis shoe to flop off. Trying to keep her cool, Monica kicked the shoe off and continued to the freezer to get the ice. Sheila waited silently at the kitchen table for Monica to wrap her ice in a towel, put on the house shoes that were by the back door, and examine the back of her foot.

"Monica, I'm so sor—"

"Bitch, just be quiet! You done just about worked my last nerve, and you ain't been here that long. Fall back!"

That shut Sheila's ass right up. Monica was a tad on the demanding side, but she'd never talked to her in that tone before. Sheila wanted to say something, but for reasons even she didn't understand, Monica scared the hell out of her. Even if she wasn't scared, she couldn't think of a snappy comeback in time anyway, so she did as she was told and fell back. After about five minutes of silence and Monica giving her dirty looks, she finally joined Sheila at the table and got down to why Sheila was there in the first place.

"I need you to help me out with something," Monica

began in a matter-of-fact tone like she dared Sheila to say she wouldn't do it.

"What is it?" Sheila did not feel like the Monica drama, but she figured if she just agreed to do whatever she wanted, she could leave and not hear from her again.

"James keeps asking about you, and he wants to know if you're down with a threesome. I told him you would do it," Monica closely watched Sheila's reaction.

Monica had spoken to James about a threesome when she was at his house the night before, but he said he didn't want anything to do with it. Since she stopped by his house that day, she had to find some way to have sex with him again if this pregnancy thing was going to work. She had taken two pregnancy tests so far and both came up positive, but she wanted to be one hundred percent sure before she visited her gynecologist.

"I'm not getting into that with you. Find someone else; you know his wife is my boss," Sheila said with her arms folded across her chest. For the first time, Sheila was seeing just how crazy and deranged Monica really was.

Monica came around the table and stood close to Sheila. She bent down so that the two were face to face.

"You'll do it," she whispered, "because if you don't, every step you take I'll be right in your ass. Trust and believe that life for you will be nothing wonderful when I'm done with you."

"Monica, what are you going to do? So what you sent pictures to the job? Your bedroom is in the background, and they weren't even clear shots," Sheila responded, feeling confident all of a sudden. She tried to play the same role Monica was playing and hoped that Monica would be somewhat intimidated.

"Dear Sheila, a lot of shit has changed," Monica said while

walking circles around the table. Her facial expression seemed to turn sinister as she told Sheila exactly how she planned to mess her life up if she didn't help her get pregnant by James.

"The photos I sent you were that way because I knew you would underestimate me. I have photos of you giving him head and everything. I can take your picture and put it anywhere I choose—even email them to Jazz if I wanted to take it to that level. How much of a job will you have then?"

Trying to hold her ground, but close to breaking down, Sheila was determined not to be a part of the nonsense. Jasmine was looking out for her in a major way even though she already violated her by sleeping with her husband. She couldn't bring herself to cross Jasmine again, and was damn near about to cry. She couldn't understand how Monica could act the way she did and not care about the lives of the people she was hurting.

Monica took her seat across from Sheila and waited for her to reply. In Monica's mind she couldn't take it far enough to get Jasmine. She wanted her as much as she wanted her next breath, and she was determined to have her by any means necessary. Sheila would be the perfect source to get Jasmine to leave James, and she figured she would have James's child so they could both have him in common. Sick and twisted? Yes, but she didn't care and was getting fed up because it was taking too long to get what she wanted.

"How do you plan to get James to come by? He's obviously happy at home. Jasmine came in the office today looking like he put some serious work in this morning," Sheila said hoping to throw Monica off.

Monica almost laughed. "You let me worry about that," she said, smirking. "Just be ready when I set up the meeting. I'll call you the day before. Now leave, your presence is making me feel sick."

Sheila wanted to grip Monica's ass up, but she decided it

wasn't worth it. Monica could call until the cows came home. Sheila would be changing her phone number the very next day, and would be staying at her mom's house during her leave of absence from work. Monica was crazy, and Sheila decided to let her be crazy all by herself. Not wanting to reveal how she would pull off her disappearing act, Sheila readied herself to leave.

"I need a ride home," Sheila said to Monica on her way to the door.

"There's money on the table in the living room. Call a cab, and wait outside for it. I want you gone before I start getting pissed."

Sheila just gave Monica a look like she couldn't believe how she was acting and walked away. In the living room Sheila found about two hundred dollars sitting on the table next to receipts from Neiman Marcus and Strawbridge's. It only cost about seven dollars for her to get home, but Sheila opted to take the whole two hundred. Instead of calling a cab, she walked until she found one. Calling her sister over to help her with her son once she got home, she gave her sister half the money to tell Monica she wasn't there no matter how many times she called. Sheila knew getting away from Monica wouldn't be easy, and she needed her sister there just in case she needed backup.

Before morning, Monica was ringing Sheila's phone off the hook. Sheila didn't think she would be calling that soon, but she did take her money and instantly regretted it. Between Monica's calls she called the phone company, but it was after hours, and she would have to wait until nine the next day to do anything.

Sheila told her sister as much as she could without incriminating herself, and her sister decided that she didn't care how many times Monica called, she would have to get over it and move on.

"Hello, can I speak with Sheila?" Monica asked in her sweetest voice. She was calling to set up some time with Sheila for the next night, hoping she could get her to help persuade James into having the threesome.

"She's not available, can I take a message?" Sheila's sister replied just as nicely. She knew it was Monica from her calling the house before, and whatever reason her sister had for not wanting to talk to her was a good enough reason for her not to like her. There was something about Monica that she couldn't place her finger on, but she knew it wasn't good.

"What do you mean she's not there? I suggest you find out where she is and have her call me back!" Monica screamed into the phone, frustration wrinkling her brow already.

"Excuse me?" Sheila's sister had to look at the phone to make sure she heard right.

"I said Sheila needs to be contacted ASAP," Monica came back with even more attitude. She didn't know who the girl was on the other end, but she did know she didn't want to talk to her.

"You need to get a better attitude before calling someone's house!" she said and hung up.

Monica was pissed. She almost dropped her phone in the tub she was so mad, and she slipped while she was getting out, damn near breaking her ankle. She didn't know who answered the phone at Sheila's house, but she didn't play those games and would be over there in a flash if Sheila didn't answer the phone.

Sitting on the edge of the bed, she dialed Sheila's number again, and this time she was ready. Sheila didn't know who she was dealing with, and Monica would make her life a living hell if she didn't act right. The phone rang ten times before Sheila's sister answered again.

"Put Sheila on the phone!" Monica demanded from the other end.

"Bitch, please! When you learn some manners, call back," and she hung up again.

This was just pissing Monica off more, and it took a lot for her not to go over to the house and snatch this woman up. Dialing the number one more time, she decided that if Sheila didn't get the phone, her life would be hell from there on out.

From Crazy To Insane

Three weeks had gone by, and Monica still hadn't heard a word from Sheila. When she called the office, a temporary assistant answered the phone, informing her that Sheila was on an indefinite leave of absence. Monica had been trying to keep her cool, but this was the last straw. Getting dressed in a sweat suit and sneakers and pulling her hair back into a ponytail just in case she had to whip someone's ass, she got in her car and raced over to Sheila's apartment to see what the problem was.

Double-parking her car in front of the building and not giving a damn that she was holding up traffic on a busy intersection early on a Saturday afternoon, she took the stairs two at a time all the way up to Sheila's third floor apartment. Knocking turned to practically trying to break the door down as Monica screamed and hollered for Sheila to show her face. She figured Sheila was inside hiding from her.

Monica was making so much noise in the hallway that Sheila's neighbors started to come out in the hall to see what all the ruckus was about. After all, Sheila didn't exactly live in the ghetto, and it was normally quiet in the overpriced, working class renters' apartment building. Monica kicked and banged on the door for a half hour, thinking Sheila would come out eventually. She was so into it that she didn't see one of Sheila's neighbors walking toward her.

"Ma'am . . . Ma'am, are you looking for someone?"

Monica turned around to stare at the elderly Caucasian guy standing a few feet from her. Almost doubling over in laughter, she tried to control her smile as she stared at him. He reminded her of the cartoon character named Mr. Burns off *The Simpson's* television show, teeth and all.

"Would I be banging on this door like a madwoman if I weren't looking for someone?" Monica asked, her smile disappearing. After thirty minutes of kicking and banging, she decided if Sheila hadn't come to the door by now, she wouldn't be.

"Well, Ma'am," the senior citizen responded like he was getting an attitude, "it's just that you're making a lot of noise, and some of us are trying to sleep."

"Does this look like the face of someone who gives a fuck?" she asked him, looking him dead in his eyes. "I'm not here for you, so take your old wrinkled ass back to your apartment before you write a check your half rich ass can't cash."

"Your attitude is not necessary, young lady. I was just simply stating . . ."

"Simply stating what?" Monica replied, approaching the elderly man like she was going to strike him.

"That you need to take that *hood* shit back to the *hood;* this is a peaceful building and . . ."

"Old man, save it! I do what I want when I'm ready. What are you going to do to stop me?"

"I . . . I'm going to call the police," Sheila's neighbor responded, taken aback by what Monica said.

"Yeah, you do that. I'll be waiting right here for them," Monica shouted at his turned back as he shuffled down the hallway and into his apartment.

She could hear him making the call to the police department and perched her tired body into one of the chairs to wait for the cops to get there. Periodically she would see the guy poke his head out the door to check if she was still sitting there, and she almost had to laugh.

"I'm still here, you old bastard, and I'm not leaving until the cops come!" He would just snatch his head back into the apartment and slam the door, disgusted by Monica's actions.

Not even ten minutes later, who but Officer Hill and Monica's other favorite officer of the law, Officer Collins, came strolling up the hallway to investigate the situation. Looking at Monica like he wasn't sure if he knew her, Officer Hill proceeded to knock on the neighbor's door to see what happened.

"Someone report a disturbance?" He asked the frail old man. He looked visibly shaken, and was afraid to step foot into the hall.

"Yes, that woman right there," he said pointing at Monica, "was making all kinds of noise and threatened me when I asked her to stop." Monica just sat there with a smirk on her face.

"Ma'am, is this true?" Officer Hill responded, taking a closer look at Monica. As he got closer to her, he recognized her, and smiled in spite of the situation.

"No, Officer, it isn't. I'm just waiting for my sister to get home. This guy seems to get nervous around black people or something," she replied, smiling seductively at the cop. He remembered the night they spent together and started blushing.

"That's a lie!" The elderly man spat out between his dentures. "She was kicking the door and everything. Look at it, you can still see her footprints on it." Everyone looked at the door at the same time, and there were scuff marks on the bottom half of it. Monica just laughed softly to herself.

"Officer, those marks were on that door when I got here. My sister was supposed to meet me here, and I've been waiting for her for about ten minutes. That's my car double-parked out front. I haven't been here for that long." Staring at Monica's breasts and not really paying attention, Officer Hill didn't hear much of what she said.

"Sir, do you have any witnesses?" Officer Collins asked the man, reluctantly turning his gaze away from Monica.

"This is ridiculous," the neighbor said. "What do you have to do to get a good cop nowadays?" Without looking back, he walked into his apartment and slammed the door. Monica and Officer Hill stood in the hallway looking at each other and smiling. Monica was hoping they would just leave, but she was sure it wouldn't go down that way.

"And for the record," the Mr. Burns look-a-like said inching his door back open, "this is a quiet building. Take all of that ruckus back to your hood," he hollered before giving the door one final slam, clicking the locks loudly.

Both law enforcers turned to face Monica. Officer Collins couldn't even look at Monica for fear that he might snatch her up. He had dealt with her for only a short time, and she had managed to almost destroy his marriage. He too fell for the Jedi Pussy Trick, falling head over heels for the sexy vixen with amazing control of her vaginal walls.

"Hill, wrap this up; I'll meet you downstairs," Officer Collins said as he walked quickly down the hall opting to take the stairs before his good intentions escaped him. Monica hid her smirk as she turned her attention to the obviously horny Officer Hill.

"So, Ms. Anderson, how have you been?" Officer Hill said to Monica while backing her into Sheila's door. His erection, as small as it was, was pressing against her abdomen, clearly showing his intentions.

"I've been good, Officer Hill. How have you been?" Monica replied seductively, hoping he would get a call on his radio or something. She was not in the mood for him tonight, and knew it wouldn't be easy to just dis him.

"Better, now that I see you."

"How's the wife and kids?" Monica shot at him as he leaned down to kiss her neck. That caught him off guard, causing him to stand straight up.

"My wife an . . . and kids?" he stuttered, trying to remember if he ever told her about his family.

"Yes. You know, your wife Cynthia, and your kids Thomas and Jessica. How are they doing?" Monica smirked and waited for his reply as his erection faded to nothing. She got information on his background from the captain in his district. He owed her a favor, and wanted her to keep his secret from his wife, also.

"They're doing great. Thanks for asking," he replied, backing away from her and adjusting his pants. "So, are you about to leave?" he asked, already walking down the hallway toward the exit.

"Yeah, my sister doesn't seem to be home."

Looking back at the door one more time, she followed Officer Hill out the building. He waited for her to get into her car and pulled up beside her in his squad car. Lust was jumping off him like fleas on a dog as he stared at Monica, trying to think of a way to get over to her house.

"You go on ahead. I'll follow you to make sure you get home safely," he said, staring at Monica's painted lips. Monica almost laughed at his attempt to get a booty call.

"No, it's cool," she replied through the window, "I'm not going straight home, but I'll call you when it's okay to stop by."

"Don't wait too long," Officer Hill practically begged. "I don't think they have a twelve step program for getting over beautiful women."

Instead of responding to his lame advances, Monica pulled off as quickly as possible, jumping on the first exit she saw, not knowing exactly where she was heading. She wanted to get away from Officer Hill as quickly as possible. It was a nice Saturday afternoon, and she did not feel like his bullshit or his thirty seconds of so-called *lovemaking*.

Skipping her exit, she decided to go shake things up at the Cinque household. She was interested in seeing how the two would act knowing they were both separately sleeping with her, but neither knowing about the other. She thought maybe she could talk to James about that threesome on the sly if Jasmine left them in the room by themselves. Smiling wickedly, she jumped off I-76 at the Lincoln Drive exit and made her way to the Mount Airy section of the city to stir up some shit.

Parking in the driveway, Monica got out of her car and peeped in the window on the way past. Seeing Jasmine and James cuddled on the couch gave her an instant attitude, and she almost snapped. James was stretched out on the couch and Jasmine was lying on top of him with her head on his chest, both watching television. They didn't see Monica in the window, and when Jasmine leaned up to give James a kiss, Monica's temper went from zero to sixty in three seconds.

"I know he's not hugged up on my girl," Monica said to herself while she looked in the window. "Doesn't he know she belongs to me?"

Knocking on the door like she was the police, she waited for someone to open it, hoping it would be James. Putting on her game face, she waited patiently for the lovebirds to separate and finally answer the door. She wanted to scream through the window that the same lips that were kissing James were all in her treasure chest not too long ago. She hated the fact that no matter how hard she tried to separate them, they always found a way to be together anyway.

"Who is it?" Jasmine's voice sounded from the other side of the door. She sounded frustrated, but Monica didn't care. She hoped she messed up their little make-out session because she didn't want James sleeping with Jasmine anyway.

"It's Monica," she said into the door. She didn't know how Jasmine would act to her popping up again, but she didn't exactly care either. She banged Jasmine's back out rather nicely a few weeks ago, so she figured Jasmine was aware of her capabilities by now.

"Who?" Jasmine asked not sure if she heard correctly. She swung the door open with tons of attitude.

"Hey Jazz," Monica said, acting like she didn't notice Jasmine's mood.

"What did I tell you?" Jasmine said getting right to the point. "Didn't I tell you not to be just popping up whenever you felt like it?"

"Yeah, but . . ."

"But what?" Jasmine said getting heated. She liked Monica a lot, but if she kept doing the stuff she was doing, she was going to mess up everything.

"I just wanted to take you shopping. I was on my way to the mall and I didn't want to go by myself," Monica replied, coming up with the lie quickly. She hoped she had at least one credit card on her, because if she didn't Jasmine would know that wasn't her reason for being there.

"Honey, who's at the door?" James hollered in the background. He was lying on the couch with a granite pipe waiting to serve Jasmine properly. Pissed because he told Jazz not to answer the door in the first place, he was wondering what was taking her so long to get back.

"Look, you have to go," she said to Monica, ignoring James. She wanted Monica to leave before James got up to see who knocked.

"We won't even be gone that long, just a quick trip to the mall," Monica replied, stalling for time. She wanted James to see her and wished he would hurry up.

Like he heard her thoughts, James finally got up to see what was going on. He wanted Jasmine wrapped around him in more ways than one, and he was ready to go now. When he got to the door his facial expressions went from shocked to scared as hell when he saw Monica standing there. He was just with Monica two days ago, and he still hadn't put the money he paid to her for the sex they had that night back into the account.

Monica was good, but she damn sure wasn't cheap. That night cost him seven hundred dollars, and it was getting harder to replace it. Yeah, she gave him a couple of free shots here and there, but most of the time she wanted her money up front if he wanted her to stay quiet. She was already pissed because he insisted on using a condom, and with that, up went the prices. Monica got even more pissed when he insisted on bringing his own condoms because he thought she was putting holes in the ones she had.

"Monica, long time no see," James said, feeling the heat between the two ladies.

"Hey, James. I was just asking Jasmine if she wanted to go to the mall with me. You know, sort of a ladies' day out. You don't mind, do you?" she asked James with a smirk. Blowing him up would be blowing herself up, but Monica didn't care about consequences.

"Well, we were about to . . ." James said looking down at Jasmine for support. He didn't want to be the one to say no and hoped Jasmine would say just that.

"Before you came we were . . . um . . . enjoying each other's company," Jasmine began, not caring if she hurt Monica's feelings, "so maybe next time you can call first and we can set up something, okay?"

"Are you telling me no?" Monica asked with a surprised look on her face before quickly checking her attitude. She didn't want to put herself out there just yet.

"I'm telling you maybe next time," Jasmine said, backing up so she could close the door. Monica looked like she was going to cry, but it wasn't working this time.

"Okay then, you lovebirds get back to each other. Jazz, I'll see you around."

Instead of responding, Jasmine closed the door in Monica's face with a hard thud and a loud click of the lock. Stunned, Monica stood looking at the door for about five minutes before she turned around and numbly walked to her car. She thought for sure she had Jasmine in check, especially after that last session, but now she wasn't too sure. James totally took her by surprise, and she knew she definitely would have to get him back for trying to play her.

"Hiding behind wifey," Monica said to herself angrily as she got into her car and peeled of from the curb. "She won't be yours for too much longer, James."

Not knowing what to do with herself because she was so mad, Monica rode around aimlessly trying to get her temper under control. For some reason things weren't working out the way she planned. At this phase, Jasmine should be ready to leave James, but they seemed more in love now than they did before.

Monica felt sick, and not sick like the morning illness she had been experiencing lately, either. She wanted to get pregnant, she wanted James's ass gone, and she wanted Jasmine now. Slamming on the breaks at a red light, she was fixing her mouth to curse the guy in front of her when she looked to the side just in time to see Sheila, accompanied by her mom and her son, come out of the Pizza Palace.

"This must be my lucky day," Monica said as she maneuvered her car into the right turning lane so she could pull into the lot before they drove off.

Running the red light, she pulled around the entrance and stopped next to Sheila on the passenger side of the car just as the door closed. Catching Sheila off guard, Monica had to control herself to keep from snatching Sheila through the car window. She had been trying to get in touch with her for weeks, and Sheila didn't look too happy to see her.

"Hey, Sheila, it's been awhile," Monica began with a false smile. The only thing that kept her from snapping was the fact Sheila's son was in the car.

Sex, Lies, and Videotape

"Hey, Monica, how have you been?" Sheila sat in the car feeling caged in because Monica was the last person she was expecting to see. She figured since three weeks had gone by, Monica would have found someone else to bully by now.

"Sheila," Monica responded mocking Sheila's high-pitched voice. She wasn't in the mood for pleasantries, and her face showed just that. "I've been trying to catch you for a while. Where are you on your way to?"

"Home. My son is tired after all that playing," Sheila responded, gesturing to her sleeping son in the car seat. She knew what Monica wanted, but she wasn't in the mood to give in.

"Why don't you let your son go ahead with . . ." Monica said looking passed Sheila to her mother. "Is it good to assume that's your mom?"

"Yes it is," Sheila's mom replied in the background, "and you are?"

"Please excuse me for being rude. I'm Monica. Me and Sheila are good friends from the office," Monica replied, planting a fake smile on her face. She made eye contact with Sheila, daring her to say otherwise. Sheila's mom wasn't aware of what went down with Monica, and once Monica figured that out, she used it to her advantage.

"Yeah, we worked at the firm together before I went on leave," Sheila responded unconvincingly.

"I was about to go into the mall. Want to hang out for a while?"

"I really shouldn't," Sheila began. "I need to put Devon down for a nap, and I'm a little tired myself."

"Girl, that's nonsense," Sheila's mom said. "I can put Devon in bed. You've done nothing but cater to him since you been on leave. Go ahead with your friend. You need some adult time for a while. I have your cell number. I'll call you if I need you."

Sheila was determined not to be alone with Monica ever again in life, and now her mom had made that virtually impossible.

"But, Mom, I need to . . ."

"Nonsense, now go and have a good time. Your son will be here when you get back."

Trying to cover her attitude in front of her mom, Sheila gathered her belongings and got out of the car. Before closing the door, she leaned in and kissed her son on the forehead, looking at him like that may be her last time seeing him. She didn't want to be with Monica, but knew if she didn't go, Monica's persistent ass would just keep following her until she gave in. The way Sheila saw it, if she just got it done and over with maybe Monica would leave her alone, but deep down she knew it wouldn't be that simple. She had to find a way to turn the tables on Monica, and she vowed to find a way to do just that and still have her job intact.

After Sheila got into Monica's car, her mom wasn't even out of the parking lot good before Monica was back out on the street. Sheila didn't have to ask because she knew they were on their way to Monica's house, and her thoughts were confirmed when she saw the only pink house on the block standing out from their spot on the corner. Neither said a word on the drive over, and Sheila decided she would let Monica do all the talking while she tried to figure out how to get out of the mess she just happened to become a part of.

Walking into the house a short while later, Sheila excused herself and went upstairs to use the restroom. Noticing the open door at the end of the hall, curiosity took over as she crept to the door to get a peek inside. That door was normally shut tight and locked down. Taking notice of her surroundings, she began looking at the canvas placed in the corners around the room. She knew Monica was a photographer, but she didn't know Monica painted as well.

Sifting through the stacks of paintings, she noticed that the woman on the paintings looked just like Jasmine. She knew Jasmine and Monica were cool, but not to that extent. She figured Monica was probably just lusting after Jasmine too, and painted what she thought Jazz would look like nude because there was no way her boss was bisexual. Leaving it to an assumption, she turned around to leave the room only to find Monica in the doorway watching her.

"Monica, I was just . . ." Sheila began, holding her chest from the shock of seeing Monica standing there. She hadn't even heard her come up the steps.

"Being nosey as hell!" Monica began taking a step into the room. "Find what you were looking for? From what I recall the bathroom is nowhere near this room."

"I . . . I saw the door cracked, and . . ."

"You want to know why you see Jasmine on those paintings?"

Shocked by Monica's ability to read her thoughts, she stood in silence just looking at her. Sheila knew she was in some shit before, but it was just sinking in as to how deep the shit really was. Monica was one powerful chick, and Sheila was feeling the seriousness of what was going on around her.

"Follow me," Monica said, turning from the room and going into the master bedroom. Sheila's legs felt like lead as she walked behind her, stealing glimpses at paintings of James and what looked like the guy from the hardware store in her neighborhood.

Walking down the hallway seemed to take forever as Sheila continued to take notice of the people in the paintings hanging on the walls. All of them featured Monica, but each man was different, making Sheila wonder how many men and women Monica had actually been with. Furthermore, she wondered if she bothered to use protection with any of them, because she and Monica never had.

Upon entering the room, she took a seat on the edge of the bed as Monica hooked up the camcorder that she hid behind the mirror to the television. Sheila didn't want to know what was on the tape for fear of who she might see. It was obvious that Monica got around, and Sheila was sure that she might know some of the people.

Monica took a seat beside Sheila and turned her face so they were eye to eye. Sheila thought she saw flames shooting up behind Monica's hazel eyes like she was the devil reincarnated. Too scared to move, but curious at the same time, Sheila waited to see what would happen next.

"Sheila, I'm going to show you this tape because I trust you. This recording is one of many, and what you see here can never leave this bedroom. Do you understand me?" Monica asked with a straight face. There were no traces of vengeance in her voice, but Sheila did detect a hint of sadness—maybe even weakness—that Monica wouldn't normally show. Sheila's mouth wouldn't move, so she just nodded her head in agreement.

At this point Monica was tired of the runaround. Going to Sheila was pretty much her only option, because she had Sheila tucked safely in her back pocket. If Sheila told, she would be putting herself out there, and Monica doubted that she would do that. Besides, it was becoming too overwhelming trying to hold everything in.

"I also want you to understand that if this does get out, it won't be wonderful for you. Get my drift?"

Without waiting for a response, Monica pushed the play button and stood by the window to wait until the tape finished playing. Monica couldn't watch the tape again because, in spite of what everyone thought of her, it was painful for her. She wanted Jasmine more than she wanted life, and she just couldn't seem to grab hold of her no matter how close she got. It was like someone was dangling a carrot in front of her and she just couldn't reach it.

Monica spotted Jasmine long before she slept with James. Jasmine had represented Monica's former lover, Tanya, in the murder case for her husband. Tanya and Monica, much like her and Jasmine, were seeing each other. Monica fell in love with Tanya, and her husband had to go—by any means necessary. Tanya didn't want to break it off because of the children they shared, even though Monica had more money than either of them could count.

Monica was getting restless and fed up, because just as James was doing now, Tanya's husband Marcus was sleeping with her also. Although Marcus treated Monica like a queen, he was very abusive toward Tanya, often leaving her with black eyes and broken bones. Deciding enough was enough, Monica went to Tanya's house one night to see if she could lure Marcus away. When she arrived, she found Marcus going through one of his many drunken fits, and he was beating Tanya unmercifully.

Monica used her spare key to get in, and she tried to help Tanya out. In a raging fit, Marcus than began swinging on her, leaving her no choice but to take the small revolver out of the pocket of her trench coat and *off* him right there. The one shot to the head would have done it, but Monica unloaded the gun into his face, reloaded, and finished him off until there was nothing left but a shell of what used to be his head.

Tanya broke down and Monica fled the scene, promising Tanya that she would get her the best lawyer money could buy. Before Monica could act, Tanya was appointed to the extremely sexy Jasmine Cinque. When Monica saw her it was love at first sight. She went through the motions of finding out who Jasmine was and if she was married. Getting info from her favorite judge down at the courthouse, she found out about James, later seducing him and talking him into the threesome with Jasmine. Now it was only a matter of time before she got Jazz, and hopefully without having to get rid of James permanently. Tanya quickly became a distant memory as Monica left her rotting in jail for a crime she didn't commit and made Jasmine her replacement.

Monica snapped out of her memories when she heard Sheila gasp. Sheila stared at the television with her mouth wide open in shock at the things the tape revealed. First, she saw James, Jasmine, and Monica at the hotel. Then there was Monica and James, including the two exchanging money. Then, there was Monica and Jasmine with the ice sculptures.

Sheila almost fell off the bed when she saw Officer Hill on the tape in front of the fireplace. Monica didn't know Officer Hill was married to Sheila's oldest sister because their last names didn't match.

Sheila was feeling sick to her stomach as she watched

Monica have her way with the obese mayor of Philadelphia. She almost lost her lunch when shortly thereafter a three-some, including the mayor's wife, Monica, and the mayor's daughter flashed across the screen.

Just as the tears began to form in her eyes, Monica came over and clicked the stop button on the DVD player. Sheila didn't know what to do as a steady stream of salty tears stained her cheeks and the front of her blouse. Monica seemed to be oblivious to Shelia, as she was dealing with her own pain and memories of Tanya. Breaking the monotony, she turned Sheila's face around so she could look into her eyes as she talked. She wanted Sheila to understand the significance of the situation before they moved any farther.

"Now, Sheila, I know that may have been a bit much to view at one time, but I need you to understand the caliber of what's happening here. I'm in love with Jasmine and I need your help. I don't want to blackmail James, but that may be the only way to get him out. Either that or kill him, and who wants to deal with that again?"

"What do you want me to do?" Sheila said through her tears. Monica had her on tape, and she was sure she had more than one copy.

"Not right now, but I'll need your help down the line. I just need to know that you got me on this."

"I can't do that to Jasmine. She helped me out in more ways than you can imagine. She's been good to me."

"I can get you a job better than that. I know people in high places. You can start tomorrow," Monica stated like that issue had no importance. She could just call one of the many judges she was sleeping with around Philly and have Sheila in a higher paying position the very next day.

"Monica, please, just give me some time."

"I don't have time!" Monica snapped, losing her cool for a

second. She was not in the mood to negotiate with Sheila; she wasn't asking her for help, she was telling her what she was going to do. "You will do it or else."

"Or else what?" Sheila asked, not really wanting to know the answer. Monica calmed down a little before answering because now was not the time to lose control of the situation.

"Fuck with me and find out," and with that said, she put the DVD back in its case and put it in the safe that she had built into the wall behind a painting of herself in a two-piece sheer thong set.

Sheila didn't know what to do about Monica or her pounding headache, so instead of arguing, she moved farther up on the bed so that she could rest her head on the pillow. She didn't know what to do with the information she had just received, but she knew she had to do something. Before drifting off to sleep, she took one last look at Monica standing by the window. Monica seemed to be struggling with her own thoughts, and for the first time she looked vulnerable. Sheila could understand her pain, although she couldn't understand why she had to drag so many lives into it.

For a second she saw Monica as a child, which she thought was comical because she didn't know her then. She saw Monica looking out the window dressed in a pink and white baby doll dress with her long, thick hair pulled up into two pigtails held together with pink and white flower-shaped barrettes. Holding a bunny rabbit tightly in her little arms, she seemed to be at a happier time in her life then. Sheila wondered if that was when her obsession with the color pink began.

As she stared at her, Sheila saw the teenaged Monica, braces and all. Acne covered her face and this Monica looked sad like she had no friends to speak of and was teased because of her absence of curves like the rest of the girls her age had. This Monica looked like the last thing she wanted to be was alive, and her face was etched with pain and worry for reasons unknown to anyone but her.

Then she turned into the evil, conniving adult Monica, and Sheila could have sworn she saw devil horns sticking up through Monica's wrap hairstyle. Chalking it up as fatigue setting in, she closed her eyes in an effort to stop the little man from dancing on her temple. She hoped by morning she would figure out some way to stop this madness for good.

"When did you and Monica start hanging out?" James asked curiously, trying to get the heat off him. He didn't want Jasmine to even begin to think he was involved with Monica in any way, shape, or form. He was still scraping up the money from the last James and Monica private party to put back into their joint savings account they had for their twins. Keeping her quiet was expensive, and he often wondered why he kept going back.

"We hang every once in a while," Jasmine responded, choosing her words carefully.

"Since when? You acted like you didn't know who she was when we saw her at the courthouse that day." James tried to turn his guilt into anger, not realizing that he was making a done situation worse for himself.

"I didn't recognize her then," Jasmine replied with the beginnings of an attitude. "I ran into her again after that and we exchanged numbers. We only had lunch a couple of times and she picked me up from here twice. Is that a problem?"

"Are you sure all you had was *lunch*?" James asked Jasmine with a straight face. If he could get Jasmine to say she slept with Monica again, it would lift some of the guilt off his shoulders.

"What the fuck is that supposed to mean? Are you implying that there should be something else?" Jasmine came back almost at the boiling point. She wanted to continue what they started before Monica came, but James was messing it up with his accusations.

"No, I'm just saying that Monica can be very persuasive. You act like you don't know she has the hots for you."

"How would you know, James? We only shared one night. How many times were you with her since then?" Jasmine shouted, cleverly tossing the ball back into his court.

James automatically saw that he put his foot in his mouth. He his reverse psychology didn't work, and he should have just let it go. He had been trying to stay away from Monica, but since day one he was drawn to her like a magnet. Deciding to bow out of the situation, he tried to come up with a lie to cover his ass before his cover was completely blown.

"I only see Monica in passing. A young lady that she's dealing with works near the station, and I see her sometimes when I'm on lunch break. She asks about you all the time, and once asked if you were interested in getting together for another threesome."

"And what did you tell her?" Jasmine asked with her arms folded tightly across her chest. James's story didn't add up only because she had been with Monica on more than one occasion, and the possibility of a threesome was never brought up.

"I told her that I didn't think you would do it because that's not your style. You only did it that one time because I asked you to."

"And she was okay with that?" Jasmine didn't sound convinced. If she knew anything about Monica, she knew that she didn't bend easily, and once she set her mind on something, that was it. She also wondered if James ever went back for more, because that story he told her about how they met just didn't add up.

"She didn't say anything otherwise, and it's been a while since I've seen her."

"How long has it been exactly?" Jasmine asked to see if he would lie about it. The night they got into the argument he came home without his boxers, and the only person she knows that keeps your underclothes after you've slept with them is Monica.

"A couple of weeks . . . She hasn't been coming that way for lunch lately, I guess."

"She told me you went there the night we got into the argument," Jasmine said, testing his credibility. She and Monica never discussed that night to that extent, but James didn't know they even talked like that.

"That's bullshit. I don't even know where she lives exactly besides the information she gave me to put the packet together for our threesome. I haven't looked at that since then, and that was so long ago."

"James, this conversation is over for now," Jasmine said while retreating up the stairs.

"But what happened with us making love on the couch?" James asked as his erection began to appear through his boxer shorts.

"You fucked that up when you decided to play detective."

"But . . ."

James couldn't get another word in as Jasmine disappeared up the steps and into the bathroom. He heard the shower running and thought about joining her. Deciding against it, he knew he had to figure out a way to leave the house so that he could go talk to Monica. He didn't know if Monica really told Jasmine he was over there or if Jazz was just calling his bluff, but he was getting to the bottom of this once and for all.

Racing up the stairs to grab his keys off the dresser, he walked in on Jasmine applying lotion to her skin. Trying not to stare at the beads of water still on her freshly showered skin, he slipped into his boots and searched his jacket pocket for his cell phone. Jasmine took note of all of this as she continued with her task. She was not in the mood to argue with James, but she did want to get some before she went to sleep. It wasn't often that the house was child-free.

"I'll be right back," James said without even a glance in Jasmine's direction. He was going to confront Monica before his marriage was destroyed.

"Where are you going and why are you leaving now?" Jasmine was a little disappointed. She was going to make it up to James by *putting it on him,* but he was leaving the house.

"I have some business to take care of."

"On a Saturday afternoon? What kind of business?"

"Business . . . I'll be back."

"Sure you will. Tell Monica I said hello."

Without bothering to respond, he walked out of the house and jumped in Jasmine's Blazer, hoping to throw Monica off a little because she wouldn't be expecting him in his wife's car. He had to set things straight if things were going to work out between the three of them, and he had to do it today.

Jasmine watched from the window as James pulled off in her Blazer, wondering why he didn't take his car. She didn't really think James was fooling around with Monica, but felt guilty as hell because she was. Changing the sheets and taking clothes out of the hamper, Jasmine found the pair of panties that she threw in there a few weeks ago. She took them out holding them to her nose, still smelling the faint scent of Monica's chocolate body butter.

Deciding to toss them in the trash so James wouldn't sus-
pect her of foul play, she cut them up into little pieces and
made sure they were at the bottom of the trashcan. Taking
the rest of the stuff to the laundry room, she busied herself
with washing clothes as she tried to think of a way to let
Monica go without ruffling her feathers.

Trouble With a Capital 'T

When James first met Monica, he was in complete awe of how sexy she was. Standing outside of The Grill, a fast food restaurant that serves ninety percent of the businessmen and women in Central Philadelphia, he spotted Monica at one of the tables outside eating alone. After placing his order, he contemplated going outside to talk to the pretty-in-pink vixen dining alone. He and Jasmine were going through *it* at home, and even though he never really entertained the idea of stepping out of his marriage, if he did, Monica would be perfect.

Hesitant at first, he stood to the side while his food was being prepared, just watching her eat. She took petite bites of her grilled chicken salad as she simultaneously sipped homemade lemonade and flipped through her copy of *Complex* magazine. She had the cutest heart-shaped lips, the bottom slightly fuller than the top.

Watching her movements, James thought she made eating almost look sensual even when she looked up a couple of times, catching him glancing her way. Her facial expression didn't change as she looked back down at her magazine and continued to enjoy her meal. James noticed that her salad was almost gone, and he wished the cooks would hurry up so he would have a reason to go over to her. As if reading his thoughts, his number was called and he made his way through the crowded restaurant and outside just as Monica was preparing herself to leave.

"Is this seat taken?" James asked, flashing his most charming smile. His smile was what attracted Jasmine to him.

"No, and actually I was just leaving," Monica said as she pushed the remainder of her salad to the side and searched her pocketbook for her car keys.

"You can't leave . . . I mean, please stay. Your company is appreciated."

Monica looked at James—his physique, his jet-black wavy hair and goatee connected perfectly on his smooth face, his eyes that looked like pools of warm caramel that made you just want to strip down to nothing and dive into them. The handsome man intrigued Monica.

"No thank you, maybe next time," Monica replied as she dropped a twenty on the table and walked away.

James was speechless as he watched her in silence, her sway hypnotic. James almost ran after her, but knew if he did it would just scare her off. When he finally sat his tray down, he noticed that the gentleman at the table next to him was looking at Monica, too. They both smiled at each other in recognition, and James settled down to eat his lunch.

The following day Monica was seated in the same spot, looking at the same magazine, eating the same meal. This time James had already ordered, and instead of asking her permission, once his food was done he went and sat down at the table with her. Monica looked up from her magazine, no indication of a smile present. James began cutting his grilled chicken into bite-sized pieces, totally ignoring the look of disdain on her face.

"I don't remember offering you a seat," Monica began, clearly annoyed. Although the man in front of her intrigued her, she didn't like the fact that he took the initiative. To her that showed signs of being pushy and inconsiderate, and she didn't tolerate that.

"Oh, I do apologize. It's just that all of the other tables are taken, and I figured sitting next to someone as beautiful as you would make all of the other men here jealous," James responded with a lazy smile. He could have easily occupied one of the tables where other men were having lunch alone, but he wasn't trying to get with them.

Monica already knew who James was from her little investigation the day before. After taking the liberty of doing a background check on Tanya's sexy lawyer, she was surprised to find out the handsome man at lunch yesterday belonged to her, and devised a plan to get next to her through him. She had to make him think she wanted him badly if she had any chance of meeting Jasmine outside of the courtroom. James was sexy, but Jasmine was a dime. Monica knew if she got the chance she would turn Jasmine out in more ways than she could handle.

"Flattery will get you everywhere," Monica flirted back openly. "What's your name?"

"James . . . James Cinque, and you are?"

"Monica."

"Monica what? I gave you both names, so now it's your turn."

"Monica will do for now," she replied with a slight smirk, satisfied that this was the correct James Cinque from T.U.N.N. The last name was not common, so she knew it had to be him.

"Okay Miss 'Monica will do for now'," James joked, "What inspires you? What do you do for entertainment?"

"A little of this, a little of that," Monica responded flirtatiously. She thought James's gullible ass was going to be easy as she picked at her salad.

"Cute . . . real cute. Well, what do you do for a living? Or does the answer remain the same?" Instead of responding, Monica placed a business card on the table. James picked it up, taking in the fancy script and pleasant smell like the cards were sprayed lightly with Breathless by Victoria.

"*Specializing in You.* Are you independently contracted or what? What exactly do you do?" James asked as he stared at the black card complete with a long stem pink rose and lettering of the same color. The card looked very chic but classy, just like Monica and completely unlike his wife's boring business cards that the firm supplied her with.

"I'm a photographer," Monica offered without further explanation.

"Family portraits, children, pets," James inquired getting a sexy laugh from Monica. "Please, elaborate for me."

"I photograph stars for several different magazines. *Essence, Complex, Sister 2 Sister, Ebony, Vibe,* things like that. I also paint and sell my work for high dollars."

"Wow," James said taken aback by Monica's forwardness. "So how do I go about getting a private session?"

"A private session, huh? Is that a wedding band I see on your finger?" Monica asked, already knowing it was.

"One has nothing to do with the other," James replied, trying to avoid the question. "How can a nice brother like myself take a sexy woman like you out to dinner?"

"Sorry," Monica replied. "I don't frolic with the talent. Have a good day, Mr. Cinque."

Without waiting for a response, Monica dropped another twenty on the table and left as quickly as she came. Looking down at the business card, James saw that she wrote her home number on the back of it. Tucking the card inside of his wallet, James wrapped his lunch to go and made his way back to the office.

Slamming on the breaks, James almost ran a red light as thoughts of Monica clouded his memory. He was clearly intrigued by Monica's beauty, but now he couldn't help but think that bringing her into his marriage was a huge mistake. He thought back on the threesome with his wife and wondered if she and Monica ever got together after that. He also thought about all the times he and Monica had unprotected sex and wondered what exactly he would do if she did get pregnant. How would he explain it to Jasmine? That threesome happened well over six months ago. The amount of money he spent on her was already an issue Jasmine could not find out about, and he was set on ending what they had today.

Pulling up to Monica's door, he parked behind her convertible and walked quickly through the closed door. Monica was elated that Jasmine came to see her until she saw James exiting the vehicle. Wondering what the purpose of his visit was, she took the steps two at a time, hurrying to answer his persistent banging on her cherry wood door.

"Why are you banging on my door like you're the police?" Monica said as she swung the door open.

"We need to talk," James replied coldly as he brushed past her, not waiting to be asked inside.

James missed the dirty look Monica gave him as she slowly closed the door and made her way to the sofa. She had just taken a pregnancy test, her third in three weeks, to confirm that she was still pregnant and the test worked. She had a gynecologist appointment in the morning that she was dying to get to. She was planning to share her good news with

Sheila once she woke up, but James's unexpected visit deterred her for a second.

"What do we need to talk about, James?" Monica inquired, already bored with his presence. She thought briefly about waking Sheila up and having that threesome just to make sure she was really pregnant, but she decided to wait. Just in case she wasn't pregnant she would need him to come by again.

"Monica, I can't do this anymore," James began while pacing back and forth in front of the couch. He knew if he sat down he wouldn't get anything said. Sitting too close to Monica was dangerous at a time like this. He needed to keep a level head to get this done.

"You can't do what, James? How many times are we going to go through this?" Monica asked as she stood up and pressed her body against his. "Are you starting to feel guilty again?"

"Did you tell Jasmine I came over here to talk about her when she made me mad that night?"

"I haven't seen Jasmine in a long time," Monica began, trying to see where he was taking this. "Why? What did she tell you?" Monica asked, taking her seat again because she was starting to feel sharp pains in her side that took her breath away.

James didn't want to put it out there if it wasn't said, and chalked it up as Jasmine trying to call his bluff. He would deal with that once he got home, but for now he had to break things off with Monica.

"She didn't tell me anything. I wanted to know if you opened your mouth to her."

"Well, I didn't." Monica said between breaths. The pains in her abdomen were getting sharper, causing her breath to come in spurts.

"Good, keep it that way. I just came here to tell you that we have to chill. I can't see you anymore. Things at home aren't right, and being here is not going to . . . Monica are you okay?"

James was so into his story he didn't see Monica doubled over in pain on the couch until he turned to look at her. His back was to her, and he was mainly focused on how to get things with Jasmine back on track. She was clutching her stomach with tears streaming down her face, a pool of crimson blood forming around her on the beige sofa. James ran over to her not knowing what to do.

"Monica, it's okay, baby, I'm calling for an ambulance now," James replied while trying to hold her up and dial 911 at the same time.

"James, tell them to hurry. I don't want to lose my baby," Monica said between her tears.

"Baby? What baby?" James said as he waited for his phone to connect to the police station.

"Your baby, now hurry up," Monica replied, as the circle of blood grew larger beneath her.

James explained the situation to the cops, and he talked to Monica once they were on their way. He was shocked because he was just thinking about what he would do if Monica was pregnant and here she was. As cruel as it may sound, he hoped deep down that the baby didn't make it. That way he wouldn't have to explain his adulterous ways to his wife.

By the time the ambulance showed up, Monica was laid back on the couch barely able to move. James did what he could to keep her comfortable, but he was getting more nervous by the second because of the amount of blood on the couch and on the floor in front of it. The ambulance walked in and checked Monica's vitals as they questioned James on what happened.

James tried as best he could to explain what went down as they wheeled Monica out to the truck. He heard Monica, as low as her voice was, telling the EMT to hurry because she didn't want to lose her baby. They jetted away from the house, moving as quickly as they could through the evening traffic hoping they could make it in time. Monica had lost a lot of blood and was miscarrying as they spoke.

Not knowing what to do as the ambulance pulled away, James turned back to the house so that he could clean the mess up. When he walked in, he saw Sheila standing up the top of the steps with tears in her eyes.

"I didn't know you were here," James said, surprised to see Sheila. The last time they got together they were in a very compromising position, and it made him feel a little uncomfortable with her in the room.

"We were just talking and I dozed off," Sheila replied, not wanting James to know that she heard bits and pieces of what they were talking about. She thought she heard Monica tell James she was pregnant, but by the looks of things she might not be for long.

They stared at each other for a while, James taking a seat on the arm of the chair to collect his thoughts. How could he ask Sheila what she heard without putting his business out there? Rubbing his temples with his fingertips he breathed in deeply, the smell of blood catching in his throat and almost choking him. Deciding to just play it out and see if Sheila would talk, he moved the conversation to the next subject.

"Look, about the last time I was here," Sheila began suddenly feeling like she had to cover herself. She didn't know what James thought of her, and she wanted to tell someone what she knew before it killed her.

"Don't worry about it. Let's just clean this up. I don't want her to come home to this mess."

Without words they both grabbed towels and cleaners and got the mess up as best they could. They couldn't do anything about the blood on the couch, but they made sure the floor was spotless, and threw the soaked pillow away so that Monica wouldn't have to deal with it when she got home.

Sheila went back and forth in her mind about whether she should tell James about the videotape as he drove her home. She had taken one from the wall safe that Monica had left unlocked, and it was now burning a hole in her pocket. He didn't look her way once, his eyes appearing glazed over as the tragedy played repeatedly in his head. James was going through his own shit, and was praying hard that the baby didn't make it. After dropping Sheila off, he went home to talk to his wife, deciding that would be the last time Monica saw him.

By the time Monica arrived at the hospital, they had to take the three-month-old fetus from her and give her a blood transfusion to help her survive. She was carrying in her tubes, and they caught it just in time. If she had waited any longer, her tubes would have burst, killing her in the process.

Pulling into his driveway a half hour later, James walked slowly up to his front door after noticing his bedroom light was still on. Debating whether he would share what just happened with his wife, he put his key in the door, not really knowing how to handle the situation. Figuring it would probably be best if he just came clean, he took the long trek to his bedroom to clear the air between him and his wife once and for all.

When he walked in, Jasmine was sleeping quietly under the covers. James saw that she had fallen asleep with the television on because the house had to be pitch black and quiet for Jazz to get any kind of rest. She said it was so she could hear the kids, but James knew better. Smiling for a second at how beautiful his wife was, he had to wonder again how everything went wrong. They had been soul mates since day one. She gave him what he asked for without any questions,

and never really gave him a reason to step out. The issues
they had were minimal and could have been worked out had
he been a little more patient with her.

Turning off the television and light and turning on the
radio, James got into the bed and wrapped himself around
his wife as sounds of Luther's "So Amazing" started to play
from the radio. Jasmine snuggled up closer to him as he
began to sing the chorus softly into her ear.

*Love has truly been good to me. Not even one sad day or minute
have I had since you've come my way. I hope you know I'd gladly go
anywhere you take me. It's so amazing to be loved. I'd follow you to
the moon in the sky above . . .*

"Jazz, I'm so sorry I hurt you baby. I never meant to."
James was trying to control his tears as he talked to his wife.
He knew she was no longer asleep because she was crying as
well. He felt her tears splash against his arm. Baby, I know I
messed up. I just need to you help me. I need you to be here
for me. I can't do this by myself. You and the kids complete
me."

"James, it's okay. I'll never leave you, baby. I want this to
work just as much as you do, but I need the truth. I need to
know what happened when you left here. I need to know
everything from day one."

*Got to tell you how you thrill me. I'm happy as I can be. You have
come and it's changed my whole world. Bye-bye sadness, hello mel-
low. What a wonderful day. It's so amazing to be loved. I'd follow
you to the moon in the sky above . . .*

As the quiet storm played on the radio, James told Jasmine
everything about Monica from day one, leaving out the money,
the baby, and a few other details that he didn't think Jasmine

could handle. He knew he was still telling lies, but it felt good to get some of the stuff off his chest. He was determined to be done with Monica and get his family back on track. Afterwards they held each other until they both fell asleep, making promises to each other to work it out the best they could.

It's so amazing to be loved. I'd follow you to the moon in the sky above . . .

Finders Keepers, Losers Cry

Monica had been in the hospital for three weeks trying to recover from the loss of her child and her near-death experience. James and Sheila didn't show their faces, and it was taking a toll on her mentally and emotionally. For the first time since Monica was a teenager, she truly felt alone in the world. In fact, ever since her mom had passed away—rather, since her mom's life was taken—it seemed as if no one in the universe cared about her.

Her depression only made her condition worse, and the doctors didn't see any sign of life in her outside of the healing of her body. All Monica did was cry day in and day out, and she wouldn't eat, so the doctors had her tube-fed so her body could get some type of nourishment. Her weight was at an unsightly low, almost making her look skeletal as she pitied herself for not taking the time to make things right in her life.

She slept most of the day, fighting off nightmares of her uncle and her sister's father molesting her as a teenager and the unforgettable incident from the tenth grade with Keith and his friends. Every man she cared even remotely about always ended up hurting her, breaking her heart.

Monica wallowed in self-pity day after day to the point where the doctor suggested she seek counseling so she could better deal with her anxiety and bouts of depression. Monica was falling apart at the seams, unlike the Monica that everyone knew.

On her last day at the hospital, after she signed up for therapy sessions and the doctor saw that she was eating and actually keeping her food down, Monica sat in her room thinking of ways to get her life back. She knew she had to get James and Sheila back because she felt like they abandoned her, and she also had to get Jasmine before it was too late. Monica was tired of sleeping alone, and she had to move fast if things were going to work.

While waiting for her discharge papers, Monica took her time putting on the new sweat suit and sneakers one of the guards purchased for her to go home in because the clothes she came in with were soiled. All he wanted was her number and dinner, and she obliged. Anything to get the overbearing, underpaid security guard out of her face.

Watching *Jenny Jones* on television while waiting for the nurse to come back, she almost fell off the bed when she saw Sheila walk through the door. Fixing her face to say something smart, Monica thought better of it, thinking she may need Sheila to help her later on down the line. Sheila came in with a small teddy bear and flowers, her facial expression showing how nervous she was in spite of her smile.

"Monica, I'm sorry I haven't been to see you. I've been so busy with . . ."

"Sheila, it's fine, no explanation is needed. I'm just waiting for my discharge papers so I can blow this joint," Monica said as she turned her attention back to the television.

Sheila took note of how frail Monica looked, almost seeing the teenage Monica she *saw* that night. Placing the teddy bear and Monica's house keys on the bed beside her, Sheila took one last look at her before she turned to leave. Nearing the door, she turned the knob, not knowing what to do and kicking herself for coming up there in the first place.

Just as she was closing the door, she heard Monica call her name. When she looked back into the room, Monica was holding the teddy bear in her hands with tears in her eyes. Sheila waited at the door for her to speak.

"Thanks for coming up here. I really appreciate it."

"It was no trouble. Just get better soon," Sheila replied and turned away quickly so Monica wouldn't see her tears.

Once Monica was sure Sheila was gone, she held up the teddy bear and took a long look at it. Ripping the head from its shoulders, she dropped both pieces in the can next to her bed. She continued watching her show as if nothing happened. She didn't need stuffed animals; she needed Jasmine, and that's all she was concerned about.

After signing her discharge papers, she walked out of the hospital and got into the waiting cab that was to take her home. The driver tried to make small talk, but Monica just stared out the window taking in the city, everything looking new to her. To her it felt like she was in the hospital for three years instead of three weeks. She couldn't wait to get home so she could lay down in her own bed and not the hard hospital one that she had been in.

Once the driver pulled up to her house, she paid him and exited the vehicle quickly so she could hurry up to her room. Upon entrance, she could smell the stale blood in the air from her recent loss. Avoiding the stained sofa, Monica all but ran up to her room, throwing herself on the bed in a fit of tears once she got there. She couldn't understand why things weren't going her way. She briefly thought about praying, but cast the thought aside after determining God wouldn't hear her for all of the dirt she'd done.

Drifting off to sleep once her tears subsided, she thought about ways of knocking James off quickly so she could finally have Jasmine to herself. The baby wasn't all that important to her, but if all else failed, Monica decided she would try getting pregnant again as a last resort. As bad as things were going, something had to give, and she hoped it would give soon.

Monica slept well until the next afternoon, the ringing phone waking her from her slumber. Upset about the interference of her much-needed sleep but glad to be awakened from the nightmare she was having, Monica answered the phone with a groggy voice lacking any type of enthusiasm. She thought it was still morning and wondered who would be calling so early.

"This better be good," Monica barked into the phone as she struggled to sit up in her bed. She was still having slight pains in her abdomen and it wasn't easy for her to maneuver around.

"You have a paid call from an inmate held in Muncy Correctional Facility. If you attempt to use three way calling or any other features this call will be disconnected. To accept this call, press three now," the computer voice spoke into the receiver.

Monica glanced at the clock, realizing it was the afternoon, and wondered who got locked up and was calling for her assistance. She had just bailed her sister out only two months ago, and hoped she wasn't sent up again. Her sister was a petty thief, and Monica was starting to think she preferred jail to having freedom. Pressing three, she spoke into the receiver ready to hear some member of her dysfunctional family beg for help.

"Who needs my help now?" Monica spoke into the phone once the call was connected. She didn't plan on helping whoever was calling, and was going to make this short and sweet.

"You seem to have forgotten about me," the voice came through on the other end sounding angry and ready to explode.

"I forgot about who?" Monica replied, thinking her mind was playing tricks on her. She hadn't spoken to Tanya since the day she was sent up for her husband's murder almost two and a half years ago. Wondering why she decided to call now, Monica didn't hide her disbelief as they continued their conversation.

"After all we've been through you don't know who this is?" Tanya came through on the other end like she wanted to snatch Monica by her neck.

"I know who it is," Monica came back with an attitude. She was over Tanya, and didn't feel like the bullshit. What was Tanya going to do for her from prison? Besides, she had her eyes on a bigger prize and didn't plan on being distracted by anyone.

"Why am I still in here? You told me a couple of weeks, and that's it," Tanya said, sounding like she was starting to cry. "I been in here for damn near three years waiting for you to get me out of this hellhole. What the fuck is the problem?"

"What do you mean what's the problem? I told you there would be some time served," Monica came back with just as much attitude.

As far as she was concerned, she didn't owe Tanya shit. If anything, she did her a favor by killing her abusive husband. Who wants to live in fear every day for the rest of their life not knowing how their man was going to act when he got home? You can't be cute with a black eye and broken ribs. Ain't nothing sexy about it. Monica came to the conclusion that if she didn't kill him he would have killed her, and it's as simple as that. No, she didn't think about the situation she put Tanya's son in, but Monica was never good at looking at the big picture.

"So, what am I supposed to do? I didn't tell on you because I thought you had my back. I thought you loved me," Tanya screamed into the phone, her emotions getting the best of her, causing the other inmates to look in her direction. Even though she told herself she wasn't going to cry, she couldn't help it. She wanted out of the stone cage she was forced to be in, and was ready to do whatever necessary to make it happen.

"What did I tell you about trusting people? Didn't I tell you no human was trustworthy? Didn't I tell you that *you* were the only one who had your back?" Monica shot the questions at her back to back, not giving her enough time to answer in between. "You come into this world alone and you leave alone. How many times have we had this conversation?" Monica was getting frustrated with the entire scenario and was about to hang up. Her main focus was Jasmine now, and she didn't want to hear shit Tanya had to say. When was the world going to understand that it was all about Monica and what made her happy? No one else mattered.

"So you just gonna leave me here?" Tanya said in a quiet voice, not believing the turn of events. She thought Monica was her soul mate, and thought about all the nights they were wrapped around each other, professing their never-ending love. The Monica she was talking to now was a complete stranger.

"Tanya," Monica began, feeling kind of bad because she was the reason Tanya was in jail in the first place, "I'll make some calls in the morning and see what I can do for you, okay?"

"Monica, listen. I need to get out of here. I can't watch my

son leave another visit. It's driving me crazy knowing that
he's too young to understand. All he knows is he wants his
mom. He cries every time he has to leave. Can't you understand the pain I'm going through?"

Monica began thinking about her own loss and the loss of
her mother years ago. There were so many times when she
needed to talk to her mom, but couldn't. So many times she
wished she had a gun so she could stop her stepfather from
beating her mom in his drunken state. So many times she
begged her mom to leave, only for her mom to tell her it was
okay as she limped to her room after being beaten nearly un-
conscious for reasons she didn't even know. So many times
she wished she had the courage to stop him that one last
time as she watched her mother's spirit leave her body, her
attacker still kicking and punching her until she stopped
moving. Monica thought about the recent loss of her child
and how it felt to be without a mother, and for a second she
had an ounce of compassion for Tanya's situation.

Brushing back tears, she got herself together as she listened to Tanya's soft cries and her pleas to get her home to
her son. All Tanya wanted was a second chance, and she
needed Monica to help her get it.

"Tanya, please stop crying. I'll be there soon, and I'll
make some calls for you today. I'll get you home, okay?"

Before Tanya could respond, her time had expired on the
call and they were disconnected. Monica held onto the
phone long after the dial tone had stopped, and the operator was instructing her to either hang up or make a call as
tears stung her eyes. She didn't want Jasmine's situation to
turn out the same as Tanya's, or worse. Calling up Judge
Stenton, the same judge who presided over Tanya's case, she
set up an appointment to meet with him in private so they
could discuss a few things. He owed her a favor, and there
was no time like the present to cash in on it.

What I Wouldn't Do For You

James had been standing outside Monica's house for at least twenty minutes, several times resisting the urge to hop in his car and stay away forever. Hating to admit that he may be slipping again, he had called the hospital earlier just as he had for the past three weeks to check with the nurses to see if Monica was okay, not wanting to talk to her directly. Fabricating his relationship to Monica so he could find out information on her—information only privileged to family—he kept tabs on her progression the entire time, telling the nurses he was her brother from out of town.

Upon finding out that she was discharged, he took off from work early to check in on her and find out if she was still carrying the baby because he didn't have the heart to ask the nurse about it. Stopping to get soup and juice for Monica, he stood outside peering up at her windows, the sun relentless on his already chocolate skin. Finally taking a deep breath to boost his courage, he went up and knocked on the door, announcing his arrival to her home.

On the other side of the door, he could hear Monica racing down the steps. His heart beat just as quickly as her foot-steps on the hard wood floor. Waiting in anticipation for her to open the door felt like an eternity; his voice came out weak and soft when she asked who was on the other side.

Monica took a step back, pausing before opening the door. James was just the person she was looking for, and she was prepared to read him the riot act for abandoning her the way he did. When she pulled the door open, James all but jumped back, gasping out loud at the woman standing before him.

Her cheeks and eyes were sunken in and her bones showed under the once tight shirt she was wearing, Monica looked like she had been binging on coke for the past couple of days. Gone was the sexy smile and mischievous eyes. Standing before him was a Monica he didn't recognize as a million questions flooded his head at once.

"Are you going to stand there and stare at me, or are you coming in?" Monica quizzed, frustrated that he caught her looking her worst. Monica always looked her best, even at her worst, so this was a rare occurrence.

As James stepped through the open door, memories of that night flashed before his eyes, causing him to sway a little as he thought about the blood and the circumstances from which it came. Daring a glance in that area, the once blood-ied sofa was replaced with a soft butter leather sectional showing no signs of the gory scene from a couple of weeks ago.

Following Monica into the kitchen, he sat the contents in his hand down, taking a seat before his face became ac-quainted with the floor. James breathed heavily, trying to control the lightheaded feeling he was having. Monica leaned against the sink taking it all in, contemplating offering him a glass of water to ease his anxiety.

"So James," Monica said while examining her nails, "what

brought you to this side of town? I thought maybe your fingers had been broken or you had amnesia."

"It wasn't like that," James began, deciding against telling her that he had checked on her every day while she was in the hospital. "I had to keep things tight at home. Maintain balance with my own family. You know how it is."

"No, I don't know how it is! As you can plainly see, I am the only occupant under this roof. Or have we forgotten already?" Monica stated sarcastically, causing James to get on the defensive.

"Look, I didn't come here for all that . . ."

"Then what are you here for? To see if I'm still pregnant with your child?"

James didn't want to just bust out and ask her the obvious even though she had hit the nail right on the head. He was trying to be a gentleman about the situation and was determined to do just that no matter how hard Monica made it to be.

"Monica, you need to slow the fuck down," James said, all of a sudden feeling strong and taking Monica by surprise. "I heard you were out of the hospital, and I came to see if you were okay. I bought you some stuff so you wouldn't have to leave the house because I was concerned. I know you're not used to people caring about your well-being, but I can do without the sarcastic bullshit."

"I just know you done lost your mind!" Monica stepped away from the kitchen sink and toward James like she was two seconds from pouncing on him and ripping his heart out his chest with her bare hands.

"You know what, Monica?" James said, backing away from the table and making his way to the front door. "This shit is for the birds. I don't want or need the drama!"

As he walked to the door, his one step equaling about four of Monica's, he could hear her playing catch-up behind him.

Regretting turning his back to her, he hoped she wasn't running up on him with a knife or something. Monica had major screws loose, and he didn't feel like having to explain it to Jazz later. He was supposed to be at work anyway.

"James, wait," Monica said as she came up behind him.

"What?" James said, still facing the door with his hand on the knob. He just wanted to know if he was going to be a father again or not. Anything else was irrelevant.

"I lost the baby. I don't know how happy that makes you, but it damn near killed me. That's all I had to keep you near my heart, the only thing I could call mine. Someone to finally love me," Monica said through her tears. She didn't want James exactly, but knew that a child would give her unconditional love regardless if he was around or not. It would make her and Jasmine's family complete.

"All you would have done was caused problems. I don't need another kid right now, and even if you had kept it we still wouldn't have been together."

"Who said it's you I want, James?" Monica said before catching herself. If James knew she was after his wife, he would never come back over.

"Then who do you want Monica? I don't think you even know."

Without continuing the conversation, he opened the door. The brightness of the sun blurred his vision for a few seconds as his eyes adjusted to the light. Monica stood in the doorway watching him walk away, not really feeling any remorse. She knew she looked a horrible mess, and that was the only reason James resisted her, but that wouldn't be for long. Closing the door and heading to the kitchen, Monica began making a feast as she calculated how she could get pregnant by James again.

Five Months Later . . .

Pulling up to the news station, Monica let the pimple-faced adolescent park her convertible after retrieving the picnic basket from the back seat. It was a nice, fall day in The City of Brotherly Love. A slight October chill could be felt on her bare skin under the trench coat she wore, making her wish for a second that she had worn more than a thong and a garter belt. Placing her free arm across her chest, she pressed down against her erect nipples as she made her way into the building from the parking garage.

It had been a while since she'd seen James. The little scene at her house during his last visit played repeatedly in her mind as she worked at getting her appearance back to what it used to be. Her once sagging breasts were back to their perky selves, sitting at attention as they brushed against the underside of her soft pink trench coat.

Her hair was braided up in micros, set on straws with a flower on the side giving her a carefree summer look even at this time of year. Monica's thigh-high boots peeked out of her trench coat every time she took a step across the marble lobby of The Urban News Network. Every eye was on her as she walked like a high fashion model, confidence dripping off her with lots left to spare.

When she reached the desk, the security guard was speechless as he sat looking in awe at the beauty in front of him. His erection was about to break his zipper, and Monica took this opportunity to get upstairs to James's office without him knowing she was even in the building. Bending over to talk to the guard with her breasts in full view, she took control quickly before the woman she knew normally sat at the desk came back from her break.

"I need you to do me a favor," Monica said to the flashlight cop in a tone only he could hear. "I'm visiting my husband in the engineering department and I don't want him to know I'm here. Is it possible for me to get a key to his office so I can surprise him when he walks in? His name is James Cinque."

The guard couldn't answer; his tongue caught in his throat when Monica touched the side of his face, the front of his pants sporting a wide circle from his ejaculation. Passing her the keys, he couldn't take his eyes off her as she kissed him on the cheek, leaving her Revlon Passion Fruit mouth print on the side of his face. She walked slowly away from him, letting him take in all of her in as she boarded the elevator, opening her coat for him as the door was closing, giving him a frontal view of what he would never have.

The elevator took her to the eighteenth floor quickly; she stepped off the elevator thankful that no one got on as she came up. Finding James's office without a problem, she drew the blinds shut tightly so no one could look in. After she set up her candles and picnic lunch, she stretched out on the leather sofa in her outfit awaiting his arrival.

James, not paying attention to the sudden darkness in his locked office, opened the door, finally looking up at the scene. Noticing Monica mostly naked on his sofa, he closed the door abruptly, being sure to put both locks on.

"What are you doing here?" James asked, taking in Monica's smooth body stretched out before him. Gone was the skeletal Monica who was nothing more than a bag of bones the last time he saw her. What lay before him was a curvaceous ebony sister, thick in all the right places. This Monica was ten times better than the Monica before her skeletal state, her body radiating heat that he could feel from his spot at the door.

"Well," Monica said as she opened her legs for him to see the crotchless thong she was sporting, the candlelight bouncing off her pierced clit. "It's been a while since the last time I saw you and I wanted to remind you of what you were missing."

Getting up off the couch, Monica looked to make sure the mini-camera was on that she placed beside the picture of him and Jasmine he had hanging from the wall. Walking up to James, she began unbuttoning his shirt, kissing him on the neck in the process.

"Monica, what are you doing?" James came back trying to get some control over the situation, his manhood standing at attention and giving away his real thoughts.

"I'm letting you know what you've been missing."

Sliding down to waist level, Monica unzipped his pants and pulled out his thickness, marveling at the evenness of his skin tone. Circling the head with the tip of her tongue first, Monica took just the head in. James leaned against the door for support.

"Monica, we can't do this," James said weakly as the effects of the brain job he was receiving took effect. "I'm at work."

"Then that means you'll have to be quiet then, huh?" Monica replied between kisses as she swallowed James up, his seed dripping from the sides of her mouth showing his excitement.

Pushing James over to the couch, he sat down with a thud, as Monica stood over top of him, holding him by his tie. Squatting down on his length, she moved slow and then fast, contracting her vaginal muscles around his shaft, causing him to explode inside of her almost immediately.

Monica being a pro, she kept him inside of her, working her muscles until he was stiff again, bouncing up and down on him like she was auditioning for a rap video. James held on to Monica's waist as he sucked hard on her nipples, adding to her pleasure. He reached between her legs and softly tugged on her clit ring until she threw her head back in pleasure. They climaxed together, evidence of their session all over his stomach and pubic area.

Monica got up and stepped away from him, bending over to remove all of their juices from his penis with her mouth, causing him to explode in the back of her throat one final time.

Allowing James to catch his breath, she stepped over to his desk and retrieved the chilled bottle of Moet she brought for their meal. Pouring the clear liquid into two flutes, Monica offered one to James, opting to remain standing in front of him. He didn't even bother to adjust his clothes, downing the champagne like it was spring water.

Finally daring a look at Monica, his length rose to the occasion again at the sight of her. He knew he was dead wrong, especially since he and Jazz had just made love that morning. Once again he didn't use protection, and that alone had him knocking himself in the head. Turning her back to him, Monica straddled James again. With his head leaned back against the sofa, he just enjoyed the ride, deciding to worry about the consequences later.

"James . . ." Monica moaned softly. Her body movement slowing down as her orgasm approached. "Can I cum, papi?"

Instead of responding, James pumped back harder, causing Monica to almost fall off him. Motioning for her to stand up, he stayed inside of her as he bent her over his desk, recklessly driving into her, trying to hurt her purposefully. Monica was staring at the photo of him and his family the entire time, in her mind replacing James's image with her own.

"Monica," James said as he banged her back out like a madman, "make this your last time coming to my office. It's over, you hear me?" Monica took too long answering, so James drove into her harder, her breasts bouncing against the side of the desk.

"I said do you hear me?"

"Yes, I hear you. Please . . . you're hurting me," Monica came back, still surprised at James. He had never sexed her with so much intensity, and for once, she couldn't handle it.

Instead of stopping, James continued his barrage against her swollen cave, holding her up as her knees tried to buckle under her. Hitting it hard, he didn't pull out until he was about to explode, doing so all over her braids and back. Stepping away from Monica's crumpled form on the floor he stepped back into his clothes, afterwards taking a sandwich from the basket.

"Have my office back to normal by the time I get back," James threw over his shoulder as he gathered his keys and made his way to the employee shower room at the end of the hall.

Monica sat for a moment longer, gathering the feeling back into her legs. First disconnecting the camera and checking to make sure she had clear footage of what took place, she put what little clothes she had back on and straightened the office back up, leaving a sandwich and soft drink on his desk before exiting.

On her way out the door, she noticed Jasmine at the front desk talking to the old white lady that should have been there when she came in. Not wanting to be noticed, she walked quickly toward the side exit, tipping the still smiling guard on the way out, and then the valet as he pulled up in her convertible.

Screeching out of the parking garage, she sped all the way home, leaving the basket in the car as she raced to her room so she could do a headstand before any of James's semen seeped out of her. It could be her last chance at getting pregnant, and she didn't want any problems making it happen.

Reality Check

The short walk from the car to the menacing gates of the correctional facility seemed to take an eternity as the sun beat down on Monica's head. On the inside she felt like she deserved the torture because she knew she easily could have been the one behind those four stone walls, calling this place home for many years. She tried to harden her heart as she approached the desk, but her soul wouldn't allow it.

This visit wasn't like the many times she'd visited her baby sister because she had committed some petty crime. This was a matter of life, death, and the well-being of a three year old who didn't understand his mother's predicament. This was reality, coming face-to-face with the real. Her legs told her to leave, but her soul made her stay.

Approaching the desk slowly, she took in the rough faces of the security guards—both male and female, but some hard to tell the difference. While waiting her turn, she observed the impatient girlfriends, baby's mommas, and family members suffering in the sweltering waiting area in order to see their loved ones.

Women in jeans so tight she was sure they would have a yeast infection by the end of the visit sat and conversed with other females they recognized from their weekly visits to the pen. Seeing belly shirts and extravagant weaves and too much skin showing to be appropriate for visiting an inmate, Monica wondered how long they had to wait for their male counterparts to come from the prison down the street. Although Monica had never been to the female holding facility, she knew the men were housed in a separate unit.

"Who you here for?" the slightly overweight guard barked from behind the podium. Monica looked into her bulldog-like face and almost vomited on the paperwork that sat in front of her from the stench of the guard's breath. The only way she knew it was a woman was from the tone of her voice and the fact that she had breasts.

"I'm here to see Tanya Walker," Monica responded as another whiff of the guard's foul breath made her take a step back.

The guard didn't seem to notice as she searched the books to make sure Monica was on the visiting list for Tanya. Searching her purse for the identification Tanya said she would need to get in, Monica placed it on the desk while the guard called over to the holding block to have Tanya come down. Monica checked her attitude as the guard looked over her ID and then sat it on the desk as if it wasn't handed to her. Monica wouldn't show her anger. She drove too far to be turned away, and she would deal with the guard when she got back.

Taking her seat after she put her belongings in a locker and turned her twenty-dollar bill into coins so that she and Tanya could have something to eat from the snack machines, Monica sat patiently waiting to be called to the back. The woman sitting next to her was trying to keep her baby quiet.

Her skirt was so short you could see her dingy panties underneath, her outfit broadcasting legs so white from ash you
could write your name on them. Monica laughed to herself
as she remembered a joke from her childhood about the
woman looking like she worked in a flour factory.

When the guard called the name out for the woman's jail-
bird boyfriend, she hurriedly got her stuff together so she
could get up front, her body smelling like a combination of
piss and cheap perfume. Monica placed a finger under her
nose discreetly as not to embarrass the woman as she struggled with the baby and a diaper bag on her way up. Monica
was lost in her own thoughts for a second, trying to steady
her nerves. It had been over three years since she'd laid eyes
on Tanya, and she hoped she could handle being that close
to her again.

The commotion broke into her thoughts as she witnessed
two women up front having a shouting match and the
guards doing nothing to stop it. Being nosey, Monica eased a
little closer so that she could hear what the drama was about.
When she got up there, the woman who was sitting next to
her and an equally tacky ghetto queen were having a debate
about who was going inside.

Apparently both of the women were there to see the same
guy, and came to find out they were cousins. The woman sitting next to Monica had his child who only looked to be a
few months old, and the one she was arguing with looked to
be about seven months pregnant. The pregnant female
knew her cousin had a baby by him, but that didn't stop her
from testing the waters before he got locked down the last
time.

The guards sat back in amusement as the ladies went on
and on about who should get to see him. After several minutes of nonstop bickering, Monica thought the women were

going to come to blows as the one holding the child sat her baby down on a nearby chair as if the infant could hold itself up.

After seeing that, the guards decided to finally break it up, telling both the women to leave for causing a disturbance in the waiting area. The women were still going at it as they walked out the door, the pregnant one going toward the bus depot, and the other going toward the parking lot.

"Family for Ms. Tanya Walker!" the manly female guard called out, getting everyone's attention. Holding her change purse tightly in her hand, Monica walked up to the front, following the guard who was escorting her to the back.

Halfway down the hall, the two came to another waiting area where Monica was fingerprinted and checked for contraband. The bulldog-looking guard came back and told Monica to step out of her shoes and clothes so she could be searched for anything illegal that the detectors didn't pick up.

"You want me to take my clothes off?" Monica asked the guard, surprised at her request. Had she known she would be going through all this, she wouldn't have made the trip.

"All of them so I can see those pretty titties," she came back with a dirty look on her face like she wanted to eat Monica alive right there.

"Where is that in the rule book? I was never told about a strip search," Monica came back, angrily refusing to take any article of clothing off. She didn't know the law like that, but she knew she had some rights.

"Leave the girl alone, Tommy," a guard said from behind her. "Miss, put your purse in the tray and walk through the detector, please."

Thankful for the interruption, Monica was more determined to deal with the guard when she came out as she took one last look at her. Somehow she would get the info needed from one of the visitors or guards before she left. She would have a nice little surprise waiting for her once she left work.

Entering the room, Monica spotted Tanya immediately. From across the room she could see Tanya's sad expression as she sat at the table with her arms folded in front of her waiting for Monica to come over. She didn't stand when Monica approached the table, and Monica had a little salt on her shoulders because she was waiting to give Tanya a hug. Taking the seat across from her, they said nothing as they studied each other.

Prison was not going well for Tanya. Her once long, jet black hair that flowed past her shoulders in a stylish wrap was now braided into cornrows straight back off her face. Although her skin was still clear, she now sported a small, jagged scar above her right eyebrow, no doubt from a fist-fight behind these walls. Her acrylic nails that always had a fresh French manicure were now bitten down way past the cuticle, and her pretty, pedicured feet were sporting Timberland boots.

Monica resisted the urge to cry as she sat looking at her former lover. She instantly regretted having Tanya in this horrible place, but not the circumstances she was there for. Had she not murdered Marcus he would have surely murdered Tanya, putting her six feet under instead of in these human cages.

"When am I getting out of here?" Tanya spoke, skipping the pleasantries and getting right to the point, catching Monica off guard. Monica leaned back in her seat to get a good look at Tanya, not expecting their visit to go like this. Tanya was usually soft-spoken, unlike the angry woman sitting in front of her now.

"Well, I talked to the judge yesterday, and he's working on

your paperwork now," Monica said in a calm voice, still not
liking the direction their conversation was taking.

"Do what you do best, I just need to get out of here."

"What the hell is that supposed to mean?" Monica said,
her temper rising quickly.

"It means," Tanya began in a slow deliberate voice, "that I
don't care if you have to fuck him, suck his dick, and take
back shots from all of his judge friends in the same night. I
want out of this hellhole. I want to be with my son," Tanya responded, trying to control her tears. She said she wasn't
going to cry, and she was determined to hold it down.

"Well, Tanya, I'm doing the best that I can, and . . ."

"Fuck the best, Monica!" Tanya came back almost knocking the chair back. "Do you know what it's like to be in
here?"

Tanya began telling Monica how it was to have someone
tell you when and how to make every move. How privacy was
nonexistent as you showered, went to the bathroom, and
lived your life in front of five thousand other inmates. How
she had to fight the women off in the beginning because she
was what they considered "fresh meat."

She drilled into Monica's head about all the nights that
she laid in her cell and cried because she could no longer
come and go as she pleased. How she would never see her
son's smiling face. She told Monica about her fear of her son
forgetting who she was because he was only a couple of
months old when she was put away. She reminded Monica
about all the birthdays she missed, and her child's first steps.

She told her of the pain she was in when she miscarried
her second week in jail because she had gotten into a fight
with one of the other inmates, and she didn't know she was
pregnant. It tore her up carrying around a secret inside of
her because she thought Monica would come back for her,

and she had left her hanging in there to rot, not giving a damn what happened to her next.

Monica shed tears as she listened to Tanya's story, thanking God on the inside that she didn't have to go through such torture. Monica was a crazy bitch, but not half as crazy as she thought. They would have eaten her ass up on the inside, and she knew it. If she didn't know before, she definitely knew now that being behind bars and being taken away from your family was some serious shit, and she had to do what she could to get Tanya out.

"Tanya, I know sorry isn't enough, and I will see the judge again in the morning so we can speed up the process. I'll do what I can to get you out of here."

"Monica, I loved you, and you don't know how it hurt for you to do what you did to me. I'm willing to let bygones be bygones, just get me out of here."

"Tanya, I will . . . I will."

The two women embraced for what felt like an eternity as they calmed their wildly beating hearts. The two spent the rest of the visit catching up and making amends as they ate snacks from the vending machines.

Before Monica left, one of the visitors from the waiting room approached her. She had peeped the altercation between Monica and the female guard, and shared her disdain for her. On the way out she showed Monica where the guard's car was parked, and both the women slashed all four tires, getting into their respective vehicles only after the woman poured a bag of sugar into the tank of the beat-down Honda. She had already planned on messing the car up anyway because the guard had given her a hard time on her last visit, and after seeing what she did to Monica, she thought Monica would want her revenge too.

The two women exchanged numbers, both seeing that they had a lot in common from the way they dressed to the vehicles they drove, hers canary yellow and Monica's hot pink. As if the world needed two women like Monica, the women exchanged brief hugs before getting into their respective vehicles and driving away. When Monica got to the stoplight, she took one last look at the card before putting it into her glove department.

"Shaneka Montgomery, World Class Photographer. Who would have thought?" Monica responded as she sped off before the light could turn yellow, glancing at her cell phone and ignoring the thirty-seven calls she'd received from Sheila since that morning. She had to go talk to the judge, and tomorrow would be too late.

Payback's A Bitch

Breaking record speed, Monica pulled up to the judge's hideaway, searching for her key in the glove compartment before she exited her vehicle. Calling the judge before she got there to make sure he would show his face, she popped her trunk and grabbed her duffel bag with tapes of him with several women just in case she needed some extra reinforcements.

Upon entry into the judge's small house his wife knew nothing about, Monica frowned at the dusty room, opting to sit her bag in a corner where she could retrieve it later. Taking the liberty of lighting the vanilla candles she had strategically placed around the living area, Monica opened a few windows to let in some fresh air to the otherwise stale environment. From the amount of dust on the sheets she had placed over the furniture, she could tell no one had been there in months.

Removing the dust covers so it could look more like home, Monica placed them in the washing machine located in the shed kitchen so they could be ready to be put back once they left. Stomach growling a little, she instantly regretted not stopping for groceries; she grabbed one of the menus off the counter to order something to eat.

Monica turned the television on to occupy herself. She flipped through channels as she waited for her food to arrive. A few minutes later she heard a key being inserted into the door, and the judge's face appearing soon after. Not bothering to greet him, she turned back to her task of turning the channels, deciding on *Wheel of Fortune* and checking her watch to see how much longer she had to wait to eat.

Judge Stenton was a handsome man, not looking anywhere near his fifty-something years. The little patches of gray at his temples showed signs of age, but the judge in full form looked good enough to eat. Standing at least six feet five inches, the judge had to bend slightly to clear the entrance of almost any building he entered. Not quite light skinned, but not really caramel, he fell somewhere in between a golden glow and sunset, turning heads wherever he went.

The fact that he worked out five days a week certainly helped, and his use of weights and morning power walks showed in his legs and upper body. Judge Stenton was well put together, and many women were killing themselves for the chance to have one night with him. How he and Monica hooked up was not that much of a mystery, but what kept them together was a sin.

Ignoring Monica completely, the judge walked past her and up the stairs to put away his clothing in the master bedroom. Placing condoms in the drawer next to the night stand on his side of the bed, he disrobed in front of the mirror so he could check out his body in the process. Satisfied with his appearance, he jumped into the shower in no rush to find out why he was summoned by Monica. He figured she wanted a favor as usual, and he wanted to be right when it came time for her to serve him for it. He knew all too well what Monica was capable of, and his length grew just thinking about it.

Resisting the urge to satisfy himself in the shower and deciding Monica would surely do a better job, he washed quickly and wrapped a towel around his waist before going downstairs to see what Monica was doing. From the stairs he could see Monica engrossed in *Jeopardy* and snacking on vegetarian shish-kebobs. Walking up to her, he placed his lips on the butterfly tattoo on her neck and surprisingly got no reaction. Continuing his journey, he reached around to caress her breasts when Monica stood up as if he wasn't even touching her, and took her plate into the kitchen.

Confused at first, he stood there looking at her as she walked away. Walking behind her, he caught up to her bending over in front of the refrigerator as she retrieved ice cubes from the bottom of the freezer. When she stood up his erection was pressed against her back, his full length very impressive. When she turned around, he tried to kiss her lips, but she turned her head, his mouth landing on her cheek.

"What's up with you? Why the cold shoulder?" Judge Stenton asked as she squeezed from between him and the icebox, making her way back into the living room.

"I'm not here for that. We need to talk," Monica said from her spot on the couch, turning the television off and waiting for the judge to join her.

All hopes dashed of getting at least some head before they got into anything serious, the judge dragged his body over to the couch, plopping down on the cushion across from Monica, his once very full erection down to nothing. Taking a good look at Monica for the first time since he came in, he saw the sadness in her eyes.

"What's on your mind?" The judge straightened the towel

around his mid-section, suddenly conscious of the way he was dressed.

"I need you to work a miracle," Monica began without hesitation. She didn't have time to be bullshittin' with him; she needed him to be on the same page.

"A miracle like what? You already know what it's hittin' for," the judge came back, letting her know what she needed to do without actually saying it.

"It's for a friend," Monica began, choosing to ignore his underlying message. "I need you to get her out of jail."

"What she in for? Murder?" the judge asked jokingly, not realizing how close to the truth he was.

"Yeah. She's in for the murder of her husband. It's been about three years now."

Not knowing what to say and shocked that his joke was actually a serious matter, the judge sat with a numb look on his face, not knowing how to react. After all, he was only joking, and on the inside hoped she was too.

"Well, what . . . what happened?" He wasn't sure he really wanted to know.

"Her husband was abusive."

"And that's a reason to kill him? Why didn't she just leave?" he asked. He had a wife at home, and every so often he had to knock her in the head to get her to understand, but that was to be expected. He didn't see the harm in running a firm household.

"He was abusive to the point where he left bruises that took weeks to heal. Broken bones and shit like that."

"Then why didn't she leave?"

"Because I promised to save her."

"And how, pray tell, did you 'save her'?" the judge asked, trying to get to the bottom of the story.

"I killed him."

The room got silent. You could almost hear a pin drop on carpet as the two dared to take the first breath, one shocked at what was said and the other shocked having said it.

"And who is your friend?" the judge asked, not really wanting to know.

"You should know, you sentenced her," Monica stated sadly as she waited for him to search his memory for recognition.

"The Walker case?"

"Exactly."

The judge looked at Monica for a long time, not knowing what to make of her. He knew she was a freak and pleased him in every form imaginable, but he had no idea he was dealing with a possible murderess. Sweat began to form on his creased forehead; he tried to rationalize as a million questions swam through his head.

"So, you were the one that emptied the clip into her husband's face? Why did you do it? How do you know Mrs. Walker?"

"We were lovers," Monica began. "She was supposed to be leaving him to be with me. I met him first through a colleague at the art gallery, and I liked him. We fucked often, and he treated me like a queen until I met his wife Tanya. It was like love at first sight. She was a little quiet and a lot timid when we first saw each other. They had just had their first child, and she was glowing from motherhood.

"It wasn't hard to talk him into getting her to have a threesome, and after that first night she was hooked. It surprised me when she approached me the morning we were leaving the hotel asking if we could possibly get together for a private session. I agreed, not thinking much of it, but wondering how far she would go because my girl was a tigress in the bedroom. Anyway, we started hooking up, and she began telling me how she wasn't satisfied at home and how she wanted out. We would hang out all the time and Marcus didn't know because we would just tell him we were out shopping when on the real we were at my house eating each other up. Excuse my French."

She went on to tell the judge how they ended up falling in love and how Marcus became jealous of their "friendship," not wanting to share his wife with the woman he was still sleeping with. Marcus always had a problem with alcohol, and when he got drunk he would beat Tanya for things she hadn't done, or he thought she was doing, often leaving bruises for Monica to clean up. Tired of the whole situation, Monica went over to the house to lure Marcus away so Tanya could leave, and she walked up on him beating the life from her.

Monica told the judge how in that instant she went back to the day her stepfather was beating her mother in his drunken state and killed her right in front of her. Not able to distinguish the present from her past, she ran in to help Tanya before it was too late, doing to him what she wished she'd had the nerve to do to her stepfather all those years ago. Before the cops got there, Monica left the house and left Tanya there. She took the gun with her, and after cleaning her fingerprints off it, she sold it to a drug dealer just to get it off her hands.

She and Tanya had an understanding that when it came time for her to go down for the murder she wouldn't tell the investigators where the murder weapon was, so they placed her before the Honorable Judge Stenton to receive sentencing. Monica left out the part about her falling for Jasmine and abandoning Tanya for the last two and half years, figuring that was info he didn't need to help her out.

"So what exactly do you want me to do?" the judge asked, not really knowing what to make of the situation. After all, he had been having sex with a murderess, and now she wanted his help to get her naïve friend out of prison. He was also hoping she wouldn't turn on him if he declined.

"I need you to get her out. That gun has a lot of bodies on it by now, I'm sure. Just arrest the guy I sold it to, pin the gun to that murder, and set her free. It's simple."

"It's not that easy. We have to catch him in the act of a sale with a large amount of product on him, and . . ."

"I can set that up for you. To make it sweet I can get him busted right at his house where he keeps everything. You ain't said nothing but a word."

"Who is the guy?"

"Rico. I know you've been trying to get him for years. I can help you."

"How soon can you do it?" the judge said, becoming excited about catching a known felon he wouldn't otherwise be able to touch. The police department had been trying to get him for years, and putting him away would surely get him a seat on a higher court. His eyes looked like dollar signs when he turned back to Monica.

"Set it up for this weekend," he said. "I need to make a few calls."

"That can happen, but I need to know that I have your word on this. She's in jail for a crime she didn't commit, and her son needs her."

"You take care of me like you been doin', and I'll take care of you. I need to make a few calls. Be naked and ready by the time I get upstairs."

Monica went upstairs to prepare for the judge, hoping she was doing the right thing. While she bathed, she could hear the judge on the phone making connections to bring down Rico and get Tanya out of jail. Making sure her diaphragm was in properly, she laid back on the bed and waited for the judge to join her.

A half hour later he came into the room full of excitement. Monica didn't know if his energy came from the case or from her naked body as he pounded into her with an intensity she never felt before. She was thankful she didn't have to tell him to put a condom on as she watched him put on two for extra safety. Monica spent the sex session thinking of a way to hook up with Rico so they could set the plan in motion.

How To Catch A Convict

"Wassup, ma? Long time no see."

Rico had spotted Monica jogging through Fairmount Park about a week after her talk with the Judge. Monica had put the word out that she was looking for him, and as sure as gossip spreads, he found her.

"Hey Rico, how you been?" Monica asked as she caught her breath from the mile-long sprint she was engaged in. If things were going to work, she had to be absolutely irresistible, and her body had to be tight.

"I been good, ma. I hear you been trying to find me. Are you finally giving in and becoming mine?" Rico joked as they took a seat on a nearby bench so that they could talk.

"Stop playin' with me. You know you don't want me like that," Monica responded, blushing. Her acting skills were in full gear.

"Ma, I been trying to get at you since I first laid eyes on you almost five years ago. You just never wanted to give me any play," Rico came back, getting comfortable on the bench, but at the same time watching his back just in case the cops chose that day to take him down.

The cops had wanted Enrique Casarez, or Rico to everyone that knew him, for years now. They could never catch him with anything major to hold him, and everything he owned was in his mother's name, so his papers were legit. Although he lived in the Mount Airy section of Philly, he stayed on the west side where he got his hustle on and made his name famous.

Rico had West Philly on lock. Just about every block was covered with workers making his money, and he knew if he were ever caught that would be one for the books. He stayed clean, never carrying too much money or product on him just in case he did get pulled over by some hatin'-ass cop. They hated how he was able to floss right in front of them and couldn't do anything because half the police force was on his payroll.

"So, word has it that you been tryin' to find me. What's that about?" Rico quizzed, looking Monica in the eyes. His mother taught him when he was young that when you want the truth, look into a person's eyes when you ask a question. The eyes tell you what you want to know, but Monica wasn't the average storyteller and his little trick wouldn't work here.

"Well, I needed your assistance in getting some protection. You know I stay by myself, and there has been someone lurking around the neighborhood, and I want to be prepared just in case he decides my house is his lucky pick one night," Monica said with a sincere look on her face like she might really be afraid.

"Why didn't you go to the guy you got your first burner from? The one you asked me to get rid of that night?" Rico asked, still trying to make sure Monica wasn't up to any bullshit. As pretty as she was, he knew she had to have some sneaky ways about her, and he didn't want to find out the wrong way.

"He's locked up. The cops caught him for drug possession and arson. He had like ten guns in his trunk when he got pulled over, and way too much coke for him to be smoking it himself."

"I see, and you don't know anyone else to get some heat from?"

"No one I can trust, and I knew you would take care of me," Monica replied, hoping her story worked.

"If you let me, I would treat you like the queen you are," Rico said, sizing Monica up. He had been trying to get her for a while, and needed someone in his corner who he could trust with everything he owned. Monica was already established, so he knew she wouldn't be on no gold digging type mission; she would be loyal to him.

As it was known, Rico was large, but he was a good investor. He started selling drugs when he was only nineteen, making a way to put food on the table because his father wasn't about shit. Although he had graduated from high school, he wasn't making the kind of money needed to maintain a household with two other children in it. Burger King wasn't paying that kind of money.

Working for a known kingpin, Johnny Constanza, Rico was paid weekly to run packages and given his own cut to hustle for extra pocket money for being loyal to his provider. Being business conscious, Rico put away a portion of his money every time he got paid until he had enough to purchase his own package.

Seeing that he was about making a come-up, he was put on to the same connect Johnny had so he could do his thing. Rico knew it was only a matter of time before Johnny went down, and he wanted to be put on before it was too late. Soon after that, Johnny for was snatched off the street, giving Rico full opportunity to blow up, and it didn't take long.

"Rico, it's not that easy," Monica replied, happy he had played right into her trap. It was easier than she thought, and she was bursting at the seams with anticipation. All she had to do was find out how his operation worked and then she could end all this madness.

Keeping in mind the timeframe the judge gave her to make this work and knowing they were on 24-hour surveillance, she agreed to let him take her to dinner later that night so they could discuss the possibility of a future together.

Rico walked her to her car, and after making sure she was safely inside, made his way to his jeep, looking over his shoulder to make sure the feds weren't on his neck. Speeding off, he went to tie up some loose ends before going back home to get ready for his date with Monica. He knew he had to come correct when dealing with her, and he didn't want to give her any reason to think he couldn't step up to the plate. He was also feeling good because he had just broken up with his girl that morning, and snagging Monica was a major step up.

On the way back to her house, Monica called the judge to inform him that the plan was set in motion. Even though she and the judge had a sexual relationship, they were actually kind of close. Friends, if you will, and Monica knew that if anyone could help Tanya out it would be him. Most people sent up for murder got consecutive life sentences or were sentenced to death. The judge, although he still put Tanya away, wasn't hardly as harsh as he could have been. *Friends with benefits* were good to have, and Monica made sure the judge was always taken care of.

*   *   *

Over the next three weeks, Rico spoiled Monica, happy
he'd finally found someone to hold him down. Trusting
Monica with his very life, he put her on to how his operation
was ran and told her enough to satisfy her curiosity so she
wouldn't feel like she had to sneak behind his back. He
couldn't honestly tell her everything—he wasn't a fool—but
he wanted her to know that there was definitely a level of
trust there on her behalf.

Good pussy will do that to you, and Rico found himself
getting more relaxed around her and not worrying about
the feds as much. He was slipping up in a major way—exactly
how Monica had planned it.

"Rico, instead of having your money in your house, did
you ever think about hiding it somewhere else? I mean, just
in case the feds did come here. You could lose everything.
Maybe you should put it in a Swiss bank account or somewhere untraceable."

Monica and Rico had just finished round two of their lovemaking, and she was wrapped in his arms like he would
never let her go. For the first time in Rico's life he was at
peace, and it felt good. He was able to be himself around
Monica, not having to lock everything down before she got
there. He left bags of money out, not concerned that any
would be missing because in his mind his money wasn't any
of Monica's concern.

"I ain't putting my money in no bank. You can't trust
those cats," Rico replied, pulling Monica further into his embrace. His manhood was awakening slowly but surely,
preparing for round three. At that moment he didn't want
to talk about money, he wanted Monica bent over the side of
the bed with her ass in the air.

"Okay, I understand your apprehension, but I'm just saying, baby, if you at least purchased a safe you could keep it in

my house. Only you and me would know the combination, and if you were ever raided, I could pay your lawyer with no problem. At least do that for the time being until you figure something else out. It would be a much safer option for you."

Hitting on a nerve, Rico contemplated the scenario Monica laid before him, not sure what he should do.

"Let me sleep on it, ma, okay?"

"Okay, baby. I'm just looking out for you, you know."

"I know, boo. Now turn over so I can get in there," he replied, referring to her wetness. By the time Monica got done turning him out, they were dressed and at Home Depot that night purchasing a safe to take to her house. By morning the safe was stored in her living room closet, and Rico deposited a little over a million dollars in ten and twenty dollar increments into the safe. Monica made sure to keep the combination in a safe place, and after making love in front of her fireplace, they enjoyed breakfast and made a trip to the mall on him.

All this time, Rico was buying Monica little odds and ends, from clothes to jewelry. She would put it up in the hall closet for Tanya. She wanted her to be set when she got home, and not have to want for anything. Rico trusted Monica completely, and on the days he gave her his credit cards she purchased gift cards and clothes for Tanya's son, telling Rico they were for her baby sister. Not really knowing her family, he went along with it, not finding a reason not to trust his girl. After all, she would never lie to him.

Time was winding down, and Monica had just about everything set up for the bust. Rico gave her a key to his home in Mount Airy and a key to the apartment he rented in West Philly where he did business. Monica made sure he separated his money in amounts of ten thousand, giving him the excuse that it would be easier for him to keep track of. Rico didn't know that he was dividing the money up for the cops who were in on taking him down. Love will make you do crazy things, and his whole demeanor was in chill mode because he felt Monica had his back. With her by his side, nothing could go wrong.

When You Least Expect It

"Monica . . . girl, what chu tryna do to me?" Rico moaned as Monica rode on top of him. He still couldn't believe how he lucked up and got her. He had been trying to get with her for the longest, but nothing he said or did worked, and it had him wondering what he did differently now.

"Turning you out, boo, ain't that what you wanted?" Monica responded as she contracted her walls around his shaft, making it virtually impossible for him to speak. She didn't expect him to answer as she continued to work her magic on top of him. Monica made sure to double up on the protection with Rico because she didn't want any mistakes this time.

This might be the only chance she had left, and when the test came up positive, she knew she had to do whatever was necessary to hold on to it. She had to be only a few weeks since she was sure it happened at the news station, and she took the liberty of scheduling an appointment to her

OB/GYN so she wouldn't have a repeat of the last pregnancy.

Today would be the day. She had Rico spending mad cash on her, and she was doing what she could to get him to take her to his place. The feds had been watching their every move from day one. They were going to put them in separate cars when they raided the place, but once they drove off, Monica would be set free. The plan was to bust in on them having sex so he wouldn't have any guns on him.

Monica's body shook from anticipation. Tanya would be set free upon his capture, and Monica would be walking away with a nice stash because she convinced him that it was safer to hide his money in her house. Monica would be walking away with a little over a million dollars, enough to set up wonderful living arrangements for Tanya when she came home. Monica didn't want Tanya back, but figured the least she could do was provide her a lavish place to call home. The house she planned to purchase was from a guy she knew in real estate who owed her a favor, and he cut her a nice deal on a three-bedroom home in the Overbrook area of Philadelphia.

Looking at the clock across the room, Monica saw that she only had about ten minutes before they were busted, and she made sure he wasn't going to cum any until then. She had given the judge a key to Rico's place so they could get him without breaking the door down. The judge was concerned about her being nude at the time of arrest, but Monica assured him it was perfectly okay. After all, half the police force had already seen her in the buff, so what difference did it make?

The feds had already set it up for him to be picked out of a lineup for the murder by some guy they had paid off. It didn't matter that the guy didn't even know Marcus, they just needed someone to say Rico killed him. They had a jury ready to go made up of officers on the squad and all, and even the lawyer he would be appointed was in on it because they were all walking away with a nice amount of cash in their pockets. Rico's money had money, so there wouldn't be any problems dishing out the dough. Judge Stenton would be presiding over the case, and Rico was getting the death penalty by lethal injection as soon as he came in. Everybody would be eating for years off this one, and they couldn't wait.

Monica maxed out all of his credit cards in the last couple of days by paying off her house and car note, and had him purchase a cotton candy pink Ford Explorer in her name for the winter months, paid in full at the dealership. Rico was blinded by all the attention Monica was showing him, and pretty much did what she said.

At exactly two o'clock in the morning the feds started entering the house while Monica and Rico were in the room getting it on. Monica had the radio on as planned so Rico couldn't hear the front door open. They turned the lights off in the hallway so when they opened the door it wouldn't shine into the apartment. After the building was properly surrounded and they were in the house, the plan went into action. Monica pulled him into her, making him explode just as the feds kicked open the door, catching him off guard. Literally snatching him out of the pussy, Monica played her part as she screamed and tried to cover up her body. Placing Rico in handcuffs, they let Monica put pants and shoes on him as she cried fake tears asking the feds what was going on.

They took Rico down the steps and put him in the car with Monica not too far behind with the handcuffs loosely placed around her wrists for appearances. Rico went off when he saw Monica being placed in the car next to his. He was trying to tell the cops she had nothing to do with it, but no one was listening to him. As they pulled off, he twisted into the seat screaming for Monica at the top off his lungs.

Rico wasn't allowed to make his first phone call for almost two weeks after he was put in placement. His thoughts stayed on Monica, constantly wondering if she was okay. He didn't know if she was brought in, but in the back of his mind something kept nagging at him. He didn't want to think it because he was truly in love with Monica, but something smelled like a setup. He just couldn't quit put his finger on it. The thought stayed on his mind well after he went to sleep, causing him to toss and turn at the thought of his love betraying him.

When he woke up the next morning, he went through the motions of washing and getting dressed, Monica still on his mind. The way things went down was just way too coincidental. He would have never gotten caught ass-naked like that.

The thoughts stayed on his mind, damn near driving him crazy by lunchtime. When the guards came by to check their cells after lunch for count, he noticed the female guard from the day before. She was always giving him flirtatious looks, and he wondered to himself if she could get him at least one call.

"Excuse me, miss lady," Rico called to the guard as she walked by. She was sexy as hell, but he couldn't see it as he tried to make sense of his situation. The guard smiled at him, relieved that he finally noticed her. She had been walking past his cell every day since he was brought to the facility, wondering when he would notice her. Yeah, she knew it was against the rules to engage in any contact (sexual or otherwise) with the inmates, but Rico was the shit. She could definitely hold it down for him.

"You talking to me?" she asked as she flirted openly with the inmate. Rico saw this and immediately took advantage of it.

"Yeah, I had something to ask you," he flirted back as he got up from the hard mattress, flexing his muscles for her viewing pleasure. She leaned against the bars after she looked around to make sure none of her co-workers were around. One of her colleagues had just gotten fired for getting caught having sex with one of the prisoners, and she was not trying to go down like that.

"I was wondering if you could help me get a phone call," Rico said as he talked close to her ear so that no one around them could here their conversation. He breathed softly down the side of her neck before catching her earlobe between his teeth, making the guard's panties wet instantly. He knew if he got caught he would be sent to the hole, but he was wiling to chance it.

"What's in it for me?" the guard asked as she thought of ways to make it happen. She was sure she could get her cell phone or someone else's for that matter.

"What you want? It's only so much I can do in my situation, you know?" Rico said as he passed the back of his hand over her tight fitting uniform shirt, lingering around her nipples before making his way to her neck.

"Let me see what I can do, but you prepare for some me and you time once it's done," the guard said before walking away, neglecting to check the rest of the cells so she could put her plan in motion.

Almost two hours went by before the guard came back. She opened his cell door and handcuffed him before leading him to the back of the building, using the cuffs to keep up appearances. Her captain was on vacation, so while everyone was out in the yard and in the recreation room she made use of the office where no one would be able to see her.

"You can use the captain's phone, but make it quick," the guard said quietly as she locked the door behind her, keeping the lights off so no one would know they were in there. "You have to be as quiet as possible, though."

Rico was already dialing his right hand man, paying the silly-ass guard no attention. He knew he would have to twist her back out, but he had to get this phone call before she got scared on him. His partner's phone rang five times before he picked up, each ring sounding longer than the last. Rico was trying to make it quick, and so was the guard as she stepped between his legs to untie the strings on his pants.

"Yo, it's me man," Rico said into the phone, trying to control his breathing as the guard pulled his penis out of his pants and began to perform orally on him. He leaned back in the chair, making it easier for her as he continued his phone conversation.

"Rico, my nigga. Don't worry baby, I got your lawyer handling everything," Rico's man said into the phone, glad to hear from his friend. He didn't know what to do and didn't want to make any noise the night Rico got caught. He was just turning the corner to go to Rico's place when he saw the law parked outside. Watching everything from across the street, he didn't leave until he saw them put Rico into the squad car, not knowing if he had stayed a little longer he would have seen them let Monica go.

"Good looking, man. I really appreciate it. Now, this is what I need you to do . . ." Rico continued to tell his partner about the way things went down and his suspicions of Monica. His partner agreed that it sounded like a setup and told him he would keep his eyes open.

In the meantime, the guard went from giving Rico head to riding him with her back facing him. Ending the call, Rico held the guard by her hips and thrust back as hard as he could until he finally exploded. Knowing he just made a huge mistake, he pulled his pants back on, unable to look the guard in the face. He wiped his fingerprints off the phone and she straightened everything up. They made their way back to his cell quickly, Rico lying down on the cot so that he could gather his thoughts. Shit just got heated, and he was not in the mood.

Word traveled fast on the streets, and when Rico's partner went to his apartment and saw everything missing, he knew for sure his man was got. Moving fast, he passed word to another partner on his team who had family in the same jail Rico was being held in. He updated his family member on everything, giving him strict orders to only talk to Rico about what he heard.

Rico was due to see the judge in a matter of weeks, but felt like he was betrayed because he still hadn't heard anything yet. Rico stayed to himself, not really coming out of his cell except to eat. He was afraid of going down, and didn't exactly want to do the time he knew he would be facing. He had been careful not to get caught all this time, making his beliefs that Monica had set him up seem more believable. Philippe, the connect between Rico and the street, had been trying to run into him but hadn't had any luck. He knew Rico was about to be sentenced and wanted him to know what went down before it was too late, but he could never find him.

One night after a poker game, Philippe had one of the prison guards take a letter over to Rico explaining everything that he knew. The same guard who made it possible for Rico to make the phone call tucked the note into her back pocket, promising she would take it to him before she was off duty.

A couple of hours later while everyone was in the cafeteria she noticed that she didn't see Rico so decided to go up to his cell block to pass the letter on. When she reached his block, it just seemed a little to quiet for her. Something wasn't right and she couldn't quite put her finger on it as she made her way past the empty cells. Rounding the corner to Rico's cell, she almost fell out as the sight of his dead body hanging from the ceiling. Screaming uncontrollably over the radio, she called for backup as she struggled with the key, unsuccessful at getting the bars open.

Everyone was put on lockdown as guards swarmed Rico's cell, everyone crowding the bars of their own cells as Rico's dead body was wheeled through the corridor. The guard didn't know what to do, totally forgetting about the letter in her pocket. She was going to reveal to Rico that she was pregnant that very evening, but he had hung himself before she got the chance.

The night before Tanya's release, Monica had Rico's apartment cleaned out, giving all of the furniture and clothing to Goodwill. The money he kept in the three safes he had in his house went to the law, each taking their share of the pie. Monica pawned all of the jewels after taking the diamonds she wanted for herself, adding another five hundred thousand to the money she already had.

When morning came, Monica was up at the prison in the office where Tanya would be released. After about two hours' worth of paperwork and fingerprinting, they were ready to go.

When Monica saw Tanya approaching, she stood up, ready to receive a hug. Tanya acted like she didn't even see her as she walked past her and pushed the button to call the elevator. Monica, hurt and confused by Tanya's actions, walked with Tanya to the car quietly, not really knowing what to say. They drove for a couple of blocks before Monica could say anything to her, not knowing what to expect from Tanya.

"Do you want to stop for a bite to eat?" Monica asked, hoping Tanya would lighten up a little.

"I just want to see my son," Tanya replied, not taking her eyes off the road. She was glad to finally be out of that hellhole she called home for the past few years and just wanted to see her family. They didn't know she was getting out, and it would be a pleasant surprise.

Before taking Tanya to her son, Monica decided to show her the house and the car she purchased for her. Pulling up to the single-family home, she got out of the car and walked around to let Tanya out. Tanya just sat there looking at Monica and not budging.

"Monica, this doesn't look like my mother's house. I haven't been gone that long to not recognize it," Tanya said from the seat with a frown on her face.

"I know that, Tanya. This is your house, for you and your son."

Stepping out of the car, Tanya took a good look at the peach and white house with the black Acura sitting in the driveway. Walking slowly up to the house, she noticed a key taped to the mailbox of her new home. Looking back at Monica, she opened the door, not knowing what to expect. Upon entry Tanya saw that the house was fully furnished, and very tastefully. It looked nothing like her old home, and she was glad because she had no desire to go back there. Every room from top to bottom was decorated, and Monica turned the back bedroom into an office for Tanya, complete with a computer and printing system. She would show Tanya the restaurant she purchased for her the next week.

Getting back into the car, Tanya still had nothing to say, but at least she had a smile on her face. Dropping her off at her mom's, Monica decided not to stay for the reunion. Once she got home, she took a bag of money from the safe before she went upstairs, sitting it by her bed as she ran a bath. After cleansing her body, she laid down in the middle of the bed not knowing what to do with herself.

Tears came from nowhere as she reached for the bag of money. Taking a handful and throwing it up in the air the money slowly floated in the air landing on her wet skin and around her on the bed. She rolled around on the money until it stuck all over her body while she cried for reasons she didn't even know. Finally falling asleep, Monica felt a little peace for getting Tanya out, and wondered what she was going to do about her and Jasmine's situation.

The Set-up

"James, you already wore that shirt this week. Why can't you just wear a different one? What's wrong with the one you got on?" Jasmine said to James, tired of the entire disagreement. They had been arguing about that damn shirt all morning and she didn't want to hear anymore about it.

"I don't want to wear another one, I want that one. I told you I had a meeting today, and that's my lucky shirt. Every account we've ever landed at T.U.N.N., I was wearing that shirt," James replied while adjusting his tie in the mirror.

James had since put on a different top, but his irritation at the situation hadn't lessened any. He didn't really care about the shirt, he was just picking a fight with Jazz so he would have a reason to not come straight home. He was meeting up with Monica to discuss "business," and didn't want Jazz to know his whereabouts.

"Well I don't know what the hell you want me to do then, James. I apologized for not getting the shirt cleaned, what else do you want?"

"I want you out of my presence. The sight of you is sickening me," James replied, still looking in the mirror. He knew he had gone there, and was waiting for Jasmine's reaction.

Jasmine had to step back for a minute to register what she had just heard. James hadn't turned from the mirror, and that pissed her off even more. Before she knew what happened, she had taken her shoe off and aimed it toward James, the heel hitting the back of his head with a dull thud. Before he could grab the back of his head, she was already on the other side of the room.

"I know you done lost your damn mind!" Jasmine yelled into James's face as he caressed the knot on the back of his head. "I don't know who you thought I was, but if you ever mistake me for one of those flunky bitches at your job again, shit will get ugly real fast."

Walking away, she grabbed her blazer from the bed and put her shoe back on before grabbing her briefcase. James was still shocked by her reaction. He was expecting her to snap, but not like that, and he would never admit that it scared him a little bit.

"Oh, and by the way," Jasmine said before exiting the room, "the five minutes you gave me last night sickened me. Get it together because I'm tired of being a damn actress. I went to school to study law, not to fake orgasms with your trifling ass."

James didn't get a chance to respond as she exited the room. Watching her from the bedroom window, he saw her get into her Blazer and realized after she had pulled off that she didn't have the kids with her. Racing down the stairs, he stopped at the kitchen entrance, his angels sitting at the table eating breakfast while watching cartoons on the thirteen-inch color television.

"Now she know damn well I didn't have time to take these kids to school," James said as he raced upstairs to gather his stuff, hoping God would spare him a traffic jam so he wouldn't be late for his meeting.

Once he got the kids settled in the car, he searched for his cell phone and almost side-swiped a school bus as he zoomed through his neighborhood well past the speed limit. Dialing Jasmine's number, he waited until the answering machine picked up before hanging up and dialing again. It took three calls before she answered the line.

"What, James?" Jasmine said still obviously irritated.

"Why would you leave the kids with me knowing I was already running late?" James barked into the phone, getting even more frustrated at the snail's pace traffic movement.

"You should have thought about that before you changed your shirt four times," Jasmine responded nonchalantly, knowing it would get under his skin even more.

"How many times I changed my shirt is beside the point! You knew I had something to do this morning." James glanced at the clock on the dashboard and the sea of cars in front of him, the scene making him madder by the second.

"Nigga, I do that every morning, so deal with it!" Jasmine just hung up. James, hating not having the last word, dialed her number right back waiting for her to answer.

"Don't you hang up . . ." before James could finish the sentence Jasmine had already fed him the dial tone. Moving to call one more time, he looked up to see his children's school up the block and decided to call after he got them situated. He didn't like arguing in front of the kids, and was upset that they had seen him angry with their mother.

After walking the kids to their respective classrooms and giving each a hug and five dollars because he felt guilty about arguing in front of them, he jumped back in his car and raced toward the expressway. His eyes just happened to catch the reading on the gas gauge; the red arrow wasn't that far from the E. Not wanting to be any later than he already was but not sure if he would make it to the city on what little gas he had, James reluctantly pulled into the gas station, calling his boss before he got out of the car.

Fidgeting around for his wallet as he apologized repeatedly to his boss, James almost lost it as he remembered leaving his wallet on the kitchen table. Having given his last ten dollars to his kids, he thought he would go crazy as he searched frantically for a credit card, knowing he wouldn't find one in the car. Not knowing what to do, the first person he thought to call was Monica as he rested his head on the steering wheel in an attempt to calm down. Calling Jasmine instead, he waited for her to answer her phone as he rationalized what to do next.

"What, James?" Jasmine talked into the phone, sounding like she wasn't in the mood for his shit.

"I need you to come give me gas money. I left my wallet in the house, and gave the money I had to the kids."

"And I care because of what?" Jasmine came back as she entered the law firm and made her way to her office, surprised to see Sheila and not the temporary secretary who was occupying the space the week before. Jasmine had been in court all week, and didn't know Sheila was back in the office.

"Jazz, come on with the bullshit. I'm not working with a lot of gas here. What's in the tank won't get me to work," James said with desperation creeping into his voice.

"You better take a cab, my trial starts in a few minutes."

"I just said . . ." Jasmine hung up.

Not knowing what to do, James began dialing Monica's number. Before he could finish dialing, he looked up just in time to see Monica roll into the gas station at the pump next to his. Silently thanking God for looking out, he rushed over to Monica, explaining the situation he was in. She didn't

hesitate to pass over her gas card as James promised to make
it up to her later while he filled up his tank. Not having time
to talk, he gave her a kiss on the cheek and hopped in his
car, arriving at work just as the presentation for new business
was beginning. He made it by the skin of his teeth, and knew
he would hear it later, but by the time he sealed the deal and
had their newest client sign on the dotted line, all of that
would be forgotten.

Snapping her cell phone closed, Jasmine signaled Sheila
to meet her in her office so they could talk. Sheila grabbed a
pencil and paper after getting Jasmine a cup of coffee.
Stepping into her office, Jasmine held up one finger indicating she would be with Sheila after she finished her call.
While listening, she graciously took the cup of steaming liquid, silently thanking Sheila for the beverage. Sheila occupied herself by drawing little knife and bullet wounds on a
sketch of Monica as she waited for Jasmine to end her call.
Ten minutes later Jasmine hung up, finally able to talk to
Sheila.

"So, Sheila, how have you been? I didn't know you were
coming back into the office today," Jasmine said as she
searched her briefcase for the files she had placed there this
morning. She was glad to have Sheila back. Not that the secretary she had wasn't doing her job, but it's smoother when
you have someone who already knows what to do.

It had been a while since Sheila had been to work, and her
first week felt kind of awkward. Now that she knew everyone's secrets, it was harder to look at Jasmine in the face
every day and not have the urge to tell her what was really
going on. She wondered if she and Monica were still sleeping
together, and what could she do to get her out of the picture.

Yeah, Monica treated her like shit, but Sheila figured that
was the only way she knew how to show her true feelings to-

ward her. Monica could be very aggressive when she wanted something, and Sheila chalked it up as her not knowing how to express herself.

Sitting in Jasmine's office waiting to take notation for a court-ordered child support document, Sheila kept her fake smile in place while Jasmine told her all about how things were going with her and James.

I wish this chick would come the fuck on, Sheila thought to herself. She was waiting to hear from Monica, and was already developing an attitude because she hadn't returned her call yet. It was already lunchtime, and she had called Monica's cell phone at least seven times since eight that morning.

"So, what do you think I should do?" Jasmine asked Sheila in the midst of correcting notes for the document Sheila would be typing up.

"I'm not sure," Sheila responded partly because she hadn't heard a word Jasmine had said.

"Well, do you think I should go with the sexy cream dress, or the magenta pant suit? I look good in either one, but . . ." Jasmine continued, unaware that Sheila was once again paying her no mind.

"I think you should go with the cream, but why all the trouble?" Sheila asked, trying to jump back into the conversation she had missed. She wanted everything cool so when she put her plan into action everything would work to her benefit.

"Because we said some hurtful things to each other this morning, and I really want our marriage to work. This on-again, off-again relationship is not working for me. I need something more solid." Jasmine thought about the latest events in her life. She wanted things to be how they were when she and James first got married, but she didn't have the slightest idea of how to get there again.

"Maybe do something that shows you're trying to work it out. An 'I'm sorry even though it's your fault' gift."

"Please explain." Jasmine laughed as she gathered her papers on her desk. This had to be good, and she wanted to give Sheila her undivided attention.

"Well, what was the argument about?" Sheila asked again because while Jasmine was talking to her she wasn't paying her any mind.

"I forgot to get his lucky shirt cleaned for his business meeting today. He wears it every time he signs a deal," Jasmine said recapping her morning.

"Okay, since he already decided to wear a different shirt, as a gesture of kindness add two more shirts to his wardrobe. Men in James's position can never have too many button-down shirts with him having to wear suits all the time. What's his favorite sport?"

"Basketball," Jasmine said, wondering what she was getting at.

"Buy him two tickets for tomorrow night's game and make reservations for dinner at his favorite restaurant. After all that, break him off real nice and put him to sleep. He'll be fine in the morning."

"That sounds good, but when will I find time to do all that? I have to be to the courthouse in twenty minutes and . . ."

"Look, I'll go get the shirts and tickets during my lunch time. Start tonight by making him dinner to see if it'll soften him up a little."

"That may just work. Will four hundred dollars do?" Jasmine said while searching her pocket book for a MAC card so she could use the machine in the lobby.

"Sure, I'll go over to Business Men, Inc. and see what they have on sale. Maybe I can find ties to match too, and I can order tickets over the phone for the game and pick them up before I come back. I have connections so I can probably get him courtside seats," Sheila said while gathering her paperwork from the desk. She planned to spend the afternoon shopping at Jasmine's expense, and would be walking out the door right next to her.

"That'll work. How fast can you have it done? I'll be back in the office by four."

"Are you extending my lunch break?" Sheila wanted to know so that she could cover her ass if something went down.

"Yeah, take as long as you need. Just have it by the time I get back."

"I will, don't worry. Now get going. I have some calls to make."

Taking her seat as Jasmine raced out of the office, Sheila sat down to call Monica one more time before leaving. This not answering the phone thing was making her mad, especially since she found out that Tanya was out of jail. Sheila was under the assumption that Monica and Tanya were together and that's why Monica wasn't answering her phone.

Nothing could be further from the truth. Monica hadn't heard from Tanya since the opening of the restaurant she had purchased for her. Monica was too busy trying to get pregnant again by James so she could put her plan into action, and Tanya was the furthest thing from her mind. The pregnancy test she took already confirmed the obvious, but Monica wanted to be extra sure this time. It just so happened that Monica was about to call Sheila when her phone began to ring.

"Just the person I wanted to hear from. What's good with you?" Monica said into the phone like everything was cool. She wanted Sheila to come over to her house when James got there so they could have the threesome. There was no way James could resist both of them at the same time.

"I've been calling you all week. Why haven't you returned my calls?" Sheila responded, heated because of Monica's nonchalant attitude. Sheila was tired of playing cat and mouse with Monica and Jasmine. She wanted to end this nonsense as soon as possible so she could move on with her life.

"I've been extra busy, sweetie. I'm sure you understand and I am so glad you called."

"Why are you glad, Monica?" Sheila wanted to know. She was so frustrated with Monica she didn't know what to do with herself.

"James is coming here later. We can do what we talked about."

"Well, I have a better idea," Sheila said, sure of her plan.

"What can be better than what I came up with? We both know who the mastermind is on this team, Sheila."

"If it were you, you would have Jazz by now, right?" Sheila stated boldly as she listened to the silence on the other end. "That's what I thought. Now this is what we're gonna do . . ."

Sheila told Monica about the incident this morning and how Jazz planned to make it up to him. Monica shared what James told her at the gas station, and told Sheila how she got him to agree to come over there and about their episode at the news station. She didn't tell Sheila she was pregnant because she didn't want to jinx it this time, but she did want them to meet up later.

"It would be better if we did it at their house, Monica. What woman wouldn't freak over that?"

"Yeah, but what if she snapped on all of us? That would defeat the purpose," Monica said, unsure if Sheila's plan would work.

"Look, trust me. When she comes back to the office she'll do some paperwork for about an hour and it will take her an hour to get home from the city. We could already be there. Just have James take you to his house when he comes there, and let him know that you know for sure Jazz is working late."

"How will I get him to go there? He doesn't want his wife to know he's cheating, idiot."

"It's simple," Sheila said checking her attitude before she snapped on Monica. "Tell him you're fumigating your house or something. You know he has no money from this morning's incident so suggest that you go over there. Give him some head in the car or something, and he'll do it. Believe me, he'll do it."

"And what if he doesn't?" Monica said, for the first time doubting herself.

"It'll work, you know how to get shit done."

"What time should we be at the house?"

"We should be in the house getting it on by six. She'll be there no later than six thirty. I'll meet you there. After y'all go in I'll knock on the door like I'm looking for Jazz. If you can, try to keep the door unlocked so I can come in without him actually answering the door. Y'all should already be having sex, I'll just join in."

"Sounds flawless, talk to you later."

"Monica, one more thing. I need you to call your man at the ticket office. I need two courtside seats for the married couple for tomorrow night."

"Done, anything else?"

"What's James favorite food?"

"Caribbean. We always order from this place called a Taste of the Islands that's near their house."

"Okay, that sounds perfect," Sheila responded as her mind raced from one thought to the next as she put her plan in order.

"Anything else?" Monica asked, ready to get off the phone. For some reason she was a little nervous about how this evening's events would end up, and she wanted to get her head together so she would be ready for James when he arrived.

"Don't be late."

After the two hung up, Sheila went on her shopping spree, getting James's shirts and ordering dinner for Jasmine so all she had to do was pick it up later. After getting an outfit for herself, she made her way back to the office just in time to see Jasmine enter the building. Coming up behind her, they caught the elevator together as Sheila explained her plans to her.

"So, all you have to do is pick up the food from A Taste of the Islands on the way home. I put the order in and paid for it earlier. I told them you would be there by six to get it."

"A Taste of the Islands, but that's all the way on the other side of town," Jasmine complained as she inspected the shirts that Sheila picked out. Satisfied with the selection, she took a peek at the tickets for the game, impressed at the courtside seats. James would love it.

"Yeah, but it's closer to your house so the food won't get cold before you get home. You and I know there ain't no heating up Caribbean food once it's gotten cold."

"Yeah, you have a point there. What did you order?" Jazz replied while starting her paperwork. By the time she finished noting her files, she would go get the food and be home in time to put the kids to sleep and spend the night making up with her husband.

"All of James's favorites with beef patties and fruit punch on the side. I also got a bottle of mango rum just in case you decided to get creative with the fruit punch, if you know what I mean," Sheila responded like she put a lot of work into it.

"Thanks, Sheila. I really appreciate this. You're leaving right?"

"Yeah, I have to go pick up my boy. See you Monday?"

"See you Monday."

Sheila got her purse and stuck what few personal items she had inside it because she knew that would be her last day after what would be popping off that evening. She knew she would miss working for Jazz, but this was the only way she could see getting Monica off her back.

Calling Monica once she got into the car, Sheila let her know everything was a go as she dashed across town to get her son and take him to her mother's house so she could get to Jazz's house in time. Everything had to go as planned or shit could backfire in everyone's face.

Not wanting to take his children anywhere near Monica, James sighed as he came to a stop in front of her house. He'd made plans to be with Monica, forgetting that he had to pick his babies up from school. He knew Monica would have a fit, but he hoped she would stay cool in front of his children. They were sleeping in the backseat, and he hoped they would stay that way until he pulled away from Monica's door. He knew kids had a tendency to repeat what they saw and heard, and he didn't want Jazz to know he was anywhere near Monica. Ringing the bell, he stood outside the door with a sad look on his face, hoping Monica would understand his situation.

"Hey, sweetie. I missed you," Monica replied while trying to wrap her arms around his neck. He stopped her advances, and stepped back, taking a look into his car to see if Jalil and Jaden were still sleeping.

"I can't stay. I forgot I had to pick my kids up from school. Can I make it up to you tomorrow?"

"I'm leaving town tonight. Why can't we do it tonight?" Monica asked, crossing her arms over her chest and pouting.

"I just told you why. Why can't I see you when you get back?"

"Because, I want you now; I can follow you to the house, and come in after you put the kids to bed. Come on James, I need you today."

"What if Jazz comes home and catches us, then what?"

Have we ever gotten caught before?" Monica asked, getting impatient with the situation.

"No, but now could be the time."

"James, come on with the bullshit. We doing this or what?"

"Look, just follow behind me and wait until I tell you to come in."

Monica said nothing, just reached behind the door for her keys and locked the door as James made his way to his car. Following him to his house, Monica found a parking space a few houses down while James pulled into the garage and got the kids into the house.

A half-hour later, James motioned from his bedroom window for Monica to come into the house. As she walked down the street, she noticed Sheila's car pulling up into James's neighbor's driveway. Not wanting to bring attention to Sheila, she walked past and went into the house, leaving the door unlocked so Sheila could come in.

Monica found James in the kitchen standing by the sink drinking a soda. She said nothing as she walked up to him, taking the bottle from his hand and sitting it on the counter. Walking James around to the other side of the table, Monica began to undress him as she sat him in the chair by the entrance with his back to the door so he wouldn't see Sheila come in.

James took it upon himself to strip so they could get it done and over with. The last thing he wanted was for Jazz to walk in and catch them in the kitchen having sex. She would go off for sure. He had left his condoms upstairs, but it didn't matter at this point because Monica was already undressed and riding him like the true rodeo queen she was.

James melted instantly as her walls contracted around his shaft, almost causing him to ejaculate prematurely. His kids being in the house only crossed his mind once before he stepped up to the plate. He didn't lock them in the room because if something happened he wanted them to be able to get out, and normally when they were asleep, it was for the entire night. He figured he would do Monica and get her out the house before anything serious jumped off.

Taking her nipples into his mouth, James closed his eyes and enjoyed the taste and feel of her wrapped around his body. He didn't hear the door open, but Monica saw Sheila walk into the house. She turned and started riding James with her back to him as Sheila neared the kitchen.

"What's going on in here?" Sheila asked as she made her way around the table. James didn't know what to do because even though they were caught, Monica never stopped riding.

"Sheila, you know what it is," Monica said as she leaned back into James so she could take him in deeper. "Care to join us?"

James was at a loss for words as Sheila stood there contemplating whether she was going to be a part of this threesome or not. Looking at her wristwatch, Sheila knew Jasmine would be pulling up in a matter of minutes, and she was deciding if she should duck out to keep her name clear or go with the plan.

The look Monica gave her helped make her decision as she undressed and climbed up on the table positioning herself so Monica could feast. All her nervousness subsided as Monica devoured her, her legs wrapped around her head and her hands gripping the table's edge. Sheila forgot about time as Monica brought her one orgasm after the next. The trio was so into it they didn't even hear the front door open.

Revelation . . .

What's Done In The Dark

No matter how much you think you are in control of a situation, you can never prepare yourself for the unimaginable. Even the most detailed person can be shocked into speechlessness. I don't even think a word exists to describe what I saw when I walked into my house earlier. James and me had been going at it for what seemed like an eternity. Just this morning we had an argument before I left about some damn shirt he said he asked me to get dry-cleaned. I'm looking at him like what the hell? He has a closet full of shit that still has the tags on it and he's complaining about a shirt he already had on this week? Give me a break.

As the day went by my anger lessened and I decided I would be the adult and apologize. On the way home I stopped and picked up a bottle of Red Door, his favorite cologne. I topped it off with a bottle of mango rum Sheila got for me so we could make frozen drinks, and two new shirts to make up for forgetting to put his other shirt in the cleaners. He picked up the kids on the way home, so I stopped to get my feet done and a Brazilian wax just in case some wild lovemaking popped off after the kids were sleeping.

I had Sheila pick up two tickets to the Sixer's game, and they were some good seats. He would be chillin' right behind the bench, watching the game up close and personal. If any sweat dripped off one of the player's armpits, he would be able to see it from his viewpoint. I told her two tickets just in case he wanted to have a guy's night out. Wasn't that sweet of me?

Also, I knew that by the time I got off work I wouldn't have time to defrost anything to cook a decent meal so I stopped by his favorite Caribbean soul food restaurant and picked up his favorite meal. Thanks to Sheila's help, this evening would be perfect.

So it was ten after six in the evening, and when I pulled up to the door I saw what looked to be Monica's car parked a couple of doors down from my house. I didn't think anything of it, thinking maybe she was visiting someone else on the block, taking into consideration that I told her of my plans before I left the office.

After parking my car and getting all my purchases out of the backseat, I saw Sheila's car parked in front of my neighbor's driveway. Now the hair was standing up on the back of my neck, and all of a sudden I felt like something wasn't right. I refrained from dropping the bags as I moved as quickly as possible to my front door. All of the lights downstairs were on, but the upstairs was dark as hell. There was no sign of the kids besides their backpacks sitting in the corner. I knew James was home because his car was in the driveway.

My stomach was knotting up even more as I sat the bags down on the loveseat. Walking toward the kitchen, it sounded like I heard voices, and not my husband's. Hesitant at first, because I was not in the mood for any more bullshit, I damn near fainted once I reached the doorway.

On my brand new oak wood kitchen table, the shit that

cost me almost two thousand dollars because James said it had "chemistry," the place where my kids and I enjoy several meals a day, the spot where I haven't parked my ass yet because I'm trying to be a fuckin' lady was the murder scene . . .

James sat in the chair while Monica rode him with her back facing him. Sheila was sprawled out on my table like she was a dish at the Old Country Buffet, and Monica's face was so far up her ass it looked like she was touching her uterus with the tip of her tongue. James's eyes were closed, and all of them were moaning like they were at a hotel some damn where.

"What the fuck is going on here?" I said in an even tone that surprised even me. My face was as red as a Crayola crayon, and my fists were balled up so tight at my sides that my fingernails cut into my palms.

Scaring the shit out of all of them, James exploded inside of Monica from the shock, and when he pushed her up, I saw he didn't have on any protection. Sheila fell off the side of the table and crawled underneath to stay away from me when she saw the expression on my face. Monica stood looking at me with a smirk on her face that I was so damn close to knocking off.

"Jasmine, what are you doing home so early?" James said in a 'damn I done messed up' voice as he tried to cover his stiff as granite member with a potholder. The fact that he was rock hard made the situation worse.

"What the fuck is going on here? Where are my kids?" I said as I tried to keep control of my breathing. I took a few more steps into the kitchen, causing everyone that was already there to step back.

"The kids are cool, just calm down. It's not how it looks," James began in a scared voice. He knew I was about to snap, and I wondered if anyone else could sense it.

"Where are my kids, James? This is my last time asking

you," I said evenly as I made my way over to the drawer where I kept my butcher knives.

"They're upstairs. They should be sleeping," James said as he watched me pull out the two largest knives without turning my back to them. "Jasmine, just calm down and let me explain."

"You had a threesome in my kitchen with my secretary and my friend on my brand new table and you want me to stay calm? My fuckin' kids are in this house, and you want me to stay calm?"

Before he could respond, I threw one of the knives at him, grazing his thigh and sticking in the wall. Monica's smirk fell off her face like a tick off a dog as I reached into the drawer to replace the knife I just threw.

"Jasmine, fall back. Why you trippin?" Monica managed.

Instead of answering, I turned and grabbed a handful of knives and began throwing them at the trio one at a time, barely missing them. I wasn't going to really stab any of them, but they would feel my wrath.

"Jasmine, please let me explain," Sheila said from her spot behind Monica under the table. Sheila was scared as shit and feared she would be cut next, especially since she was the one who went and got all the stuff for this so called 'perfect' night. James tried to get under there with them, but there wasn't any room. Blood was running down his leg and it formed a puddle that he slipped on as he tried to join the ladies and get out of my path.

I took a good look at them looking like they were all about to shit on themselves as they cowered under the table. I didn't even have the words to say anything, and I didn't want to hear any excuses. Taking a look at them, then around the kitchen, I suddenly felt dirty. Dropping the remainder of the knives on the floor, I turned and ran quickly up the steps, not stopping until I got into my children's room. Thankfully they were still sleeping when I got there because had they

witnessed any of this evening's events I would have to definitely cut somebody up.

I didn't pack any clothes; I just scooped my babies up and
headed downstairs. When I got down there, Monica, Sheila,
and James were clothed and standing in the living room
waiting for me. I said nothing as I struggled to keep my tears
in, not believing these bitches would do me like this. I
trusted both them hoes, and they cut me deeper than any
knife ever could. Gathering my keys and my pocketbook, I
juggled the twins in both arms as I finally got the door open,
and prepared to walk down the driveway.

"Jasmine, you just can't leave like this. Can we talk?"

I turned to look at James, then the other two. Sheila
looked like she was about to pass out, and Monica wouldn't
make eye contact. James looked like he was trying to make
himself cry, but at that moment any love I had left for him
was nonexistent. I could feel the ice form around my heart
as I turned away and made the long trek to my Blazer.

James knew he was wrong, and he just stood in the doorway watching me strap the kids in. Monica was in one window and Sheila was in the other. Proud of myself for not
snapping, I got in my car and pulled off. I kept my tears in
check all the way to my brother's house by blasting my Tupac
CD because I didn't want to hear any slow jams. I didn't want
anything replacing the hate I was building up in my heart
for James. The scene in the kitchen replayed constantly in
my head. It wasn't until I pulled up into my brother's driveway that I let my tears fall.

I was a complete mess as I told him what I had just witnessed and what I had done to them with the knives. He was
ready to go over there with a nine-millimeter and off all of
them, but I talked him out of it. I put the kids in the guest-
room, and then I stretched out on the couch, contemplating
what went wrong in my life.

Epilogue

$\mathscr{B}$ack at the house, James and Monica argued as Sheila sat on the side taking it all in. She didn't know what she was going to do about money now that she had sealed her fate with Jasmine. At the same time she was glad that Jasmine found out so Monica wouldn't have any power over her anymore.

Slipping out the back door as the argument got heated, Sheila snuck by the window just in time to hear Monica tell James she was pregnant with his child. Her steps faltered a little as the revelation of what really happened popped in her head. Monica went about getting Jasmine the wrong way, and even if Jasmine were to take James back, Monica was carrying his seed.

Shaking her head in defeat, Sheila made her way to her car and pulled off, trying to come to grips with how she was going to survive from here on out. She wanted to talk to Jasmine, but knew it wasn't a good time to do so. Everything seemed like a dream as she drove on the quiet streets seemingly moving at a snail's pace. She hoped to never see Monica again, and even never would be too soon . . .

About the Author

Taking her first shot at writing a novel, Anna J. is coauthor of *Stories To Excite You*—released during the fall of 2004. *My Woman His Wife* is the first of many full length works of fiction that this proclaimed "Diva" will be putting out there for your reading pleasure.

As a full-figured model, Anna is no stranger to being in the spotlight and rather enjoys the attention. Anna is also one of the faces of The Philadelphia Writers Partnership, an editing service for up and coming authors. She resides in Philadelphia and is currently working on her next book.

THE AFTERMATH

Nobody Has To Know

As Monica felt the pain of the contractions she was having, she wondered if the pain she was enduring had been worth it. She had been in labor for ten hours now. She was getting ready to deliver the baby that she and James had conceived and the physical pain from the contractions was almost so unbearable that she began to wonder whether or not getting pregnant by James in the first place had been worth it. And while she contemplated her present plight, her mind also began to drift back to the emotional pain she had endured during her childhood and adolescent years. Monica didn't know which pain had been worse, but while the physical pain would eventually end, it seemed liked she would forever be plagued by her emotional pain from years gone by. Of all times, why during labor, was she thinking about her dirty, old, no-good uncle? She could still here his voice as if it were yesterday . . .

"Monica, open this damn door! What I tell you about locking my damn doors around here?"

Monica was on the other side, fearing for her life as she

hurriedly dressed before her drunken uncle broke the door down. She didn't want him to see that she was anywhere near undressed, knowing what would happen if he did. Finally zipping up her pants and tucking her shirt in tightly, she unlocked the door and opened it just as he was about to kick the door in.

"Who you got in this room, girl? Who you tryna hide?" Uncle Darryl said barging into the room almost knocking the frail fourteen-year-old Monica into the wall.

She stood as far away from the bed as possible not wanting to give him any ideas about them two getting in it. She didn't know how she ended up in this never ending nightmare, but she knew that when she got old enough she would leave. In her heart she vowed that a man would never touch her once she escaped. Not like this.

"I was 'sleep and didn't hear the door," Monica replied in a barely audible voice, not wanting to upset her uncle anymore than he already was.

"Let me find out you lying," he responded with a snarl. "Ain't nobody hittin' that but me, and as ugly as you is won't nobody want cha any ways. Get 'cha ass downstairs and clean that kitchen. I told you I wanted that done before I came home from work."

"Okay, Uncle Darryl, I'm right behind you," Monica stated, looking around the room for something to do so that she wouldn't have to walk past him.

"I said I want it done now. Move ya ass!"

Hesitant at first, Monica moved by him as quickly as she could, almost running. She wasn't fast enough though because when she got past the doorway, he reached out and grabbed her pants pocket, his other hand pulling her back by her shirt collar. He reached into her shirt, fondling her formations of breasts because Lord knows she didn't have any yet. Monica, grimacing from Uncle Darryl grinding himself against her and kissing behind her ear, did everything she could to hold her tears in, hoping he wouldn't try to make her go back into the room.

"Nobody betta be hittin this but me. Ya hear?" he whispered into her ear as he continued to explore her underdeveloped body.

"Yes sir," was Monica's only reply as she made her way downstairs once he released his hold on her.

For the life of her, Monica couldn't figure out what a grown man could see in her. Boys her age thought she was hideous, so she couldn't gather her thoughts on why she had to practically beat her uncle off her at least five nights a week. He would never actually penetrate, but he seemed to get off on just rubbing the head against her, and she gagged almost every time. She knew the slimy stuff he left behind was not supposed to be there, and she honestly thought the only reason he didn't actually do it to her was because it wouldn't fit.

Monica found herself on a few nights holding a mirror between her legs so that she could look at herself wondering what he saw different. There was barely any hair there, and to her it didn't look appealing, but that didn't seem to keep his mouth off it. From her sex education classes she knew what he was doing was wrong, but who could she tell? Uncle Darryl had threatened to kill her if anyone found out, and her fourteen-year-old mind believed it, so she just took the abuse and hoped he would just die one day or opt to leave her alone.

She didn't know what to do about the red bumps that hurt like hell when she went to pee, but she knew she had to do something soon because she couldn't take the itching and burning anymore.

Starting to cry, Monica wished her mom were still alive. Killed at the hands of her lover, Monica wished she had the strength that night to help her mother out. Her feet seemed to be made of lead as she watched her stepfather beat her mother until she no longer was breathing.

When the cops came, this after she had the courage to reach for the phone by the end table, her sister, Yolanda, the baby of the family, was taken to go live with their Aunt Joyce over in West Philly. Her brother, the middle child, was taken to their grandparents' house, and Monica was stuck with drunk-ass Uncle Darryl.

She didn't know if she was going to make it out alive, but knew once she did, every man from then on would pay dearly for what she went through. She thought it was over when her mom passed away, at least then she wouldn't have to worry about her sister's dad trying to sneak into the room late at night and their mom acting like she didn't know. Only it seemed now that she jumped from out of the frying pan and into a big ass fire because Uncle Darryl was bold with his shit, and the fight was no longer easy. Uncle Darryl would pay when the time was right. Him and every man after him would get what they deserve . . .